SHERIFF GUS

John D Desain

ACKNOWLEDGEMENT

The Author would like to thank Andrea Hsu Schouten
for the use of her artwork.

CHAPTER 1

Gus sighed and set down his half-full coffee cup over the head on the photograph. The idea of having to think this early in the morning always upset his stomach. Thinking about work-related matters only aggravated the circumstances. Thinking was best left to the professionals, and even they, thought Gus, were not required to think about things while eating breakfast. If only he could just stop thinking long enough, he could finish eating in a pleasant manner.

Gus tried the simplest plan, which was placing the offending picture out of sight and thus out of mind. The problem with this plan was that it was a hopelessly short-lived one. His mind was bound to stubbornly wander over the article he was trying not to think about just as a matter of course of the natural process of not thinking about it. The brain was a difficult organ to distract, and even giving it something useful to do like think about eating scrambled eggs was apparently not sufficient to distract it from thinking about all the ways to not think about that which Gus was pretending hard not to think about.

He stirred his eggs on his plate with his fork. Gus groaned at his stupid brain and gave in to it yet again. Up went the coffee cup in defeat, and once again the picture in the morning paper stared back at Gus, taunting him. You couldn't deny it was a very professionally done photograph of an extremely photogenic, blond, middle-aged man. He was dapper, physically fit, and did not appear overdressed in a well-tailored suit. He appeared perfect, and yet the picture didn't make sense to Gus. What did a successful district attorney like the man in that photograph want with the kind of a public job he was apparently shooting for?

The article made him sound like every other self-centered Ivy Leaguer with too much time on his hands. He was clearly living the good life already—married, with two lovely kids. They were very photogenic kids as well, with their combed, short, blond hair and pale blue puppy-dog eyes. Worst of all to Gus was "the wife." The article made her out to be more than just extremely photogenic. She was just short of supermom, with the two kids, hardworking husband, and charity work. No doubt they would look appealing on the upcoming campaign posters, but still none of it made a lick of sense in Gus's mind. A guy like this, with everything going for him, should play it safe and enjoy the good life in the big city. A comfortable guy with that wife and those two kids shouldn't risk everything to run for sheriff in a poor county in the middle nowhere. Sure, they had announced the plan to run months ago, but this first public appearance made it all so real. To Gus it seemed like a career move of someone incredibly stupid, and yet the guy in the photograph looked anything but.

Gus closed his eyes and rubbed his temples. Nope, the morning wasn't a good time to be thinking about problems, and that family was looking like a major one, particularly to whoever was now the sheriff—i.e., Gus, who had been elected sheriff by the good citizens of the county ten campaigns in a row. While some political animals lived their whole lives for the thrill of running for office, folks like Gus sort of eased into the elected-office circuit. Back in school Gus was never that wrapped up in learning, and he generally found time for it only due to his dad's insistence that either Gus went to class or got a red backside. When life gives you nothing but bad choices, you choose the path of least resistance; Gus went to school all the way through high school graduation.

Graduation brought a sudden end to Gus's childhood and ushered in the reality of adulthood. The reality was, adults of the county didn't live the fantasy American Dream life where each son did better than his father. Instead they lived in a slowly decaying postwar boom town. In the good ol' days, the county ran on the money brought in through the ranching industry. The Cold War years saw the city centers grow prosperous on the new economy of manufacturing. Those two eras were on their way out by the time of Gus's graduation. There weren't enough jobs in the county to go around, so Gus's dad got his son to join up for the volunteer military. He said the military would make a man out of Gus.

Gus had no idea if service ever had made a man out of him or not. He had the misfortune of serving during the non-glamorous between-war years. The service turned out to be nothing like the World War II movies Gus grew up watching. Instead service life was a life of rote boredom and predictable routine. If manhood was about doing the boring and predictable for hours on end, then the service had made a man out of Gus.

While in the service Gus trained for the military police. He left the military after his father passed away. Returning to his hometown, Gus found that there were now even fewer jobs available than before. It was then that Gus fell into a bit of good fortune. Gus's old high school friend Terrance convinced him that Gus had what it took to run for sheriff. Terrance assured him the process was easy: it was a one-party county, and no one was bound to contest Gus so long as the party bosses backed him. Terrance was a political fixer for the bosses, and he would make sure they'd arrange everything. All Gus had to do in return was play ball for the county bosses.

The law enforcement life in those early years was so much simpler. There was an instinctive understanding between the powers that be and Gus on who was to be profiled, arrested, investigated, and cracked down on and what was not to be worried about too much. The citizens had a natural understanding of their place and where they got stuck if they were found out of place. Those olden days also had good, clean, honest popular elections. Gus even liked his opponent in those days-he ran unopposed.

But the good times couldn't last forever, and the times were clearly changing. And not for the better, thought Gus. Now those old party bosses had either gone bankrupt, retired to the big city, or, worst of all, dropped dead. For the first time in anyone's memory, the county had a real political organization on the other side. The picture in the newspaper meant that for the first time in Gus's law-enforcement career he had to beat an actual person to hold his office.

Gus looked again at the photograph of his new political opponent. He wondered if this guy really understood that being sheriff wasn't that great a job. People assumed it was a prestigious job, filled with glamor, but it wasn't, as far as Gus was concerned. People tended to look at the sheriff with a sense of either nervous paranoia or blind hatred. Little old ladies would smile to you on the street and then flip you the bird when your back was turned. The old ladies' children would deflate the tires on your patrol car or shoot out your windows in a drunken act of stupidity. There was little joy in evicting the old woman from her apartment because her social security check wasn't enough to pay the bills. There was even less joy in dealing with domestic disturbance after domestic disturbance. On top of all that was the fact your fellow officers on the state and federal level loved to clarify your place in the pecking order. They took every opportunity they had to fine you for a minor infraction and write you up a ticket. Gus held the state record for most times in traffic school.

If this fancy guy in the picture was looking to gain some sense of respect, then he was running for the wrong office. The truth was, the job sucked, so why would anyone else want it? Gus drank the rest of the coffee and banged the cup down on the table.

It was clear to Gus the answer must involve those new corporations in the area. During the economic housing boom they built huge new sub-urban tracks out in the middle of the ranch land. They had plans not for ranching but for development. Inside these new suburbs, the county population was growing and expanding, with city who bought the houses out there because they couldn't afford the ones in the city. Young and middle-aged people that worked in the big city up north flocked to the new suburbs. The long-time locals all called the suburbs bitterly "the development."

The development people brought their big-city ideas, big-city money, big-city music, and, most important to Gus at this point, their big-city politics into Gus's quiet county. Of course, what they didn't bring was any real support for the actual old county community. The development dwell-ers lived in their own small corner of the world. The development people only ventured from it to take the highway north to work and play in the big city. They didn't drive into the county proper to shop and socialize; they went to the cheap box stores that now lined the highway. To those in the development, the rest of the county was like a foreign land occupied by an unwanted and unwashed horde of unwanted guests. To Gus and the old guard of the county, the feeling was mutual. You only had to look at your average local development residence to guess whose sheriff he hoped to be. He was *their* pick, not the real county people's pick.

Gus figured that the development people wanted one thing above all others: higher and higher property value. In their opinion being surrounded by locals ran counter to that purpose. The locals dragged down the school's test grades, so the development had built their own charter schools. The locals were all redneck racists who hated Mexicans and blacks since the dawn of the time. Had the development people ever driven around the county they may have noticed a fair share of the county population was actually Hispanic and African-American these days, but it never occurred to them to look. The development people thought all the locals drank, smoke, chewed, and smelled. While it was true there was entirely too much drinking and dope smoking in the county, the development people were no better. They simply brought to the county newer, flashier drugs-cocaine, heroin, meth, and designer prescription drugs. The people that were bound to purchase in the development thought they were better than the local community around them. Whether they were or weren't wasn't the point; they thought they were, and thus big changes needed to be made. Houses needed to be flipped if they were going to climb up the property ladder. Now, apparently, they were aiming to flip something else-Sheriff Gus.

Gus looked at his political opponent one last time. The photograph caption read "Lance Daniels is signing up to help clean up the county." This big-city candy-ass won't be able to hack the job for more than a month, Gus thought. That guy was used to plea bargaining down his opponents, not beating them in open court by rule of law. Lance wasn't a fighter, like Gus. He didn't have that fighter look in his eyes.

In the end, thinking in the morning had not ended up being so bad. Gus suddenly felt better about his situation. Gus was a fighter and this guy wasn't. Also, when push came to shove, the comfortable people of the development weren't fighters like the real county folks. They all lacked the killer instinct, thought Gus.

Gus finished off his eggs and hash browns. He hurried to clear the plate from the table and place it in his dishwasher. He poured the remains of his morning coffee pot into a thermos and then folded up the paper so he could keep his opponent mentally close as he headed out for another day's work. It was a crummy job in a down-and-out place, but it was Gus's job, and he wasn't about to go down without one fierce political fight.

Gus pulled his suburban truck into his personal parking place at the county law-enforcement complex. The parking place was one of very few perks. Judging by the sight waiting for him in front of his office, Gus figured the workday was going to get off on another wrong foot. There was a man asleep on the bench between Gus and the building's front door. The man was well known to Gus and was in Gus's mind totally unsuitable. If the development people's minds were going to be changed about the sheriff's office in this county, then Gus was going to have to start by cleaning up the front of his office. Particularly it needed to be cleared of the sight of this man. If only the man had been something sympathetic, like a dirty homeless vagabond, thought Gus. Instead the man was wearing the official sheriff's deputy uniform.

Gus climbed out of the truck with his thermos and paper and walked over to the sleeping man. Gus bounced the bench bottom with his foot violently until he woke the man from his slumber.

Sheriff Gus spoke sternly but in a controlled volume, "Deputy Drew, rise and shine. It is now time to work. Speaking of your work, you were supposed to be on prisoner transfer today, so why is it that I find you yet again sleeping one off on my public bench? Need I remind you to please show a minimum amount of respect for the uniform and what it is supposed to represent? If the need to pass out overcomes you in the future, I ask you kindly to pass out in front of your own home and not in my station. It is the election season, boy, and we all have to remain reputable for the good of our beloved public."

The man slowly opened his eyes and sat up on the bench. Gus had only hired Deputy Drew because he happened to be the mayor's son. An idiot and a chronic drunkard, Drew was more than qualified to hang out at a prison, but unfortunately for the community he only did so as an authority and not as one of the permanent residents. Deputy Drew finally managed a few words.

"Sorry, boss, but I won a bet with Deputy Wilson last night, and as a result he's got to do the prison transfer and I got to have a night of fun."

"Glad to hear you were both gambling on the public dime. The fun and the night are now over. I congratulate you on being too drunk to make it home, but in your drunken stupor you are actually briskly punctual to work the desk detail this morning. So get your sorry butt off my bench and inside to your desk, where, if we are all lucky, you won't be seen again until the clock strikes quitting time!"

Gus had many competent deputies that far too often went on to bigger and better positions, leaving the Deputy Drews of the world permanently in the office to help him. The best course of action would be to give Deputy Drew a vacation until the election was over, but the tremendous downside to that was that the mayor might get his wind up about it. Gus needed the mayor's support now more than ever.

Gus finally made his way inside the sheriff office. As usual he found his secretary, Lupita, already working. She was the hardest-working person in the office and was the only one in the department older than Gus. Lupita predated not only everyone in the law-enforcement complex but the actual building itself. Gus wasn't sure of her exact age, and they didn't get along well enough for him to ask. All he knew is somehow the office worked and wouldn't work without her, because in memory of anyone living it hadn't had to.

"Good morning, Lupita. Isn't it a bright and shining morning?"

"Have you seen the paper today, Sheriff?" asked Lupita, holding up the front page, a red heart drawn around the picture of Lance. Gus took the folded paper out from under his arms and held it up so she could see it.

"Then you know it is a bright and sunny day today," she chirped, "because I will soon have a brand new boss. Lance sure looks like a nice and attractive young man. I've always told you: I was here before you came, and I'll be here after you're gone. I think we both know it is almost leaving time for one of us," smiled Lupita.

Gus faked a smile. "Thank you, Lupita. You always know just the right thing to say to really get the whole sheriff station in a good mood. I hate to inform you that I am planning on remaining in this office for quite some time to come."

"You know that's what the last sheriff said too. Then one day he dropped dead of a heart attack in the bed of his mistress. Between dying unexpectedly of a heart attack in the bed of your mistress and being voted out of office, I frankly find the former a more dignified way to go."

Gus rubbed the temples of his head. "I don't remember it being his mistress; as I recall, she was only some local whore. Now unless you have anything else sarcastic to say, I will go into my office."

"Terrance is already inside your office waiting for you."

"That's not very sarcastic," replied Gus.

"Then your opinion of Terrance is higher than mine," retorted Lupita.

"Thank you, Lupita. You will always be my little ray of sunshine that starts the day," complimented Gus as he reached for the door to escape into his office.

"It is too bad your fat butt blocks my sunshine. Now don't go walking into your little office just yet; I have a note for you to read." She pulled a sticky note off her desk and handed it to Gus.

"Do I have to read it, or were you about to give me the gist of it anyways?"

"Ernie London says he needs you over at his ranch right away. He gave me detailed instructions about where to meet him. It's all in the note."

"He didn't say why I needed to come over, did he?"

"No, he just said that it was urgent and to meet him there as soon as possible."

Gus frowned at the note, grabbed it from her hands, and shoved it in his pocket. He then turned to open the door to his office.

"*Es usted un estúpido idiota.* Where the hell do you think you're going? Didn't you hear me? Ernie said it was urgent and to come right away!" shouted Lupita in a shrill voice.

Gus turned to face her one last time. "Look, I've been sheriff of this town for a long time now. I know its established residents like the back of my hand. Ernie is always imagining phantom cattle rustlers. I'll get over to his place when I'm good and ready. This is my office for a few more months. Now if you don't mind, I am going to talk to Terrance to try to make sure this remains my office."

Gus let the office door close between him and Lupita. He turned to see a grinning, happy, balding man sitting in a chair in front of his desk. Terrance and Gus had been friends for as long as Gus could remember. Terrance's family had all the right connections and Terrance had gone to all the right schools. As far as Gus could remember, Terrance didn't learn anything in those schools, but they were the type of schools where it was more important to go to them than to learn something in them. Terrance was still the county's party fixer and was generally in charge of running campaigns and finding willing candidates.

"Terrance, can you please tell me what the hell is going on?" erupted Gus, who finally got to say to someone what he had been thinking all morning.

"It's all very simple, Gus. He's your opponent. It is a bit of a shock to us all that someone has challenged your office, but it is legal. People are allowed to run against you for the sheriff's office. We didn't count on him actually showing up to run, but here he is in the flesh. But there's nothing to worry about; running against someone is almost just like running against nobody, and we've never lost to nobody yet."

Gus walked past Terrance and took a seat behind his desk. He held up the paper he was carrying and pointed to his opponent. "Well, if we're going to win, let's start with the basics of a winning plan. Who the hell is this Lance Daniels? I mean who is he in the sense of not the obvious stuff written here in the paper?"

"The boys got the rundown on this Lance fellow, but it's basically just like what the papers say about him. He's a district attorney from upstate who calls the authorities in this county a blight on the otherwise stellar reputation of this state. He says that he will clean up this county from the racism, drugs, gun smuggling, and corruption. It's the same as what's in the paper because we gave it to the paper. But as to whom the hell he really is…well, we are still trying to figure it out."

"Don't get all cute and innocent on me, Terrance. You bigwig guys got to have impressions. Heck, even I got a guess as to what is going on," grumbled Gus, who started fiddling with his thermos lid.

Terrance stood up and started pacing. "Now look, Gus. Honestly we don't know who this guy is. He doesn't have ties to the county and he certainly wasn't recruited by the power base here. From what we've been able to dig up, he doesn't have the track record of a holy crusader either. We think he's store bought, but we don't know yet who the buyer is."

"Can't you just say he's been recruited by the development? What do the day-tripping city snobs in the development have against me? I stay out of their way for the most part. I can't remember the last time I even drove into the development except to stop some idiot from beating up his wife. What are they, pro wife beating?" asked Gus.

"Like the article says, Gus, it is all about image. The development people are listening to the opposition party bosses in the capital that think the rural areas in the state are giving the state a national black eye. They say the authorities here let too many guns slip to the south and too many drugs into the cities to the north. They say we harass too many minorities and we are all a bunch of racists. I guess they figure they need to start cleaning up the county's image."

"So they want to clean up the image but not the actual causes of bigotry and racism? Nice fellows they are up in the capital. We were just doing what the guys in the capital told the boys to do—profile the criminals they told us, keep the Mexican gangs out and let them kill each other on their side of the border. I've been doing it all for years, and now they start complaining that I did what I was told to do? Hell with them. Maybe we could just appeal to all the other county people that have been here for generation after generation and let the development go fuck itself. No? OK, Terrance, you win. Why don't you tell me how to appeal to both the honest racists outside the development and the dishonest ones inside it?"

"With this!" Terrance held up a yard sign with an image of a much younger and slimmer Gus, who had a full head of hair and no overhanging gut.

"Who the hell is that?"

"That's a picture of you from your first campaign. Don't you remember him?"

"Aw shit, Terrance, everyone knows what I really look like now," pointed out Gus.

"Not the people in the development. You and I know that most of them never spend a second in the actual county sans driving to and from the city on the highway. So we control the information they receive and give them the you they want, not the you they never met. Here you are, Gus: a clean, young, white, professional-looking guy with fresh ideals and a fresh outlook on society!"

Gus didn't like the new Gus. He thought the new Gus was probably an ideological bigot and a little naïve as to where the actual corruption lay in the county. Then again, it wasn't corruption that was hard to find so much as honesty and integrity. The old Gus knew these things, but apparently he was no longer running for his office. Well, things just couldn't get worse today.

Terrance then had one more indignity to present to Gus. He reached down into a bag and pulled out a white cowboy hat. "Gus, we can't have you seen without the hat for the rest of the election season. The polls say that the people love a sheriff in a cowboy hat. The hat is the perfect image, and it also perfectly covers up that gray and receding hair. I'm telling you, we snowball forty percent in the development, all the old boys in the county will still back you, and bam! We win this thing going away."

Gus picked up the hat. He looked at the sign. It was embarrassing to him. What happened to that young man in that photo? It felt like he existed a lifetime ago.

"All right, Terrance, you can tell your boys I'm still playing ball. Let's hope this young Gus right here wins your election. If the two of you can keep me in my little stately court here for three more years, I'll keep playing the game."

"Don't forget: a week from now I've scheduled a debate on the issues with this Lance guy at the charter high school in the development. It will be your big chance to meet and beat the opposition," smiled Terrance triumphantly.

"Which Gus is supposed to show up and debate?" asked Gus, pointing to the young Gus. "Don't answer that just yet, Terrance. I got official sheriff work to do. You know, cops-and-robbers work. There's trouble at Ernie's ranch. It ain't exactly glamorous, and you don't need a cowboy hat to do it, but it has been paying my bills a long time. I'll catch you and new Gus later."

With that Gus went over to young Gus and pretended to shake his hand. He placed the cowboy hat firmly on top of his head and adjusted it, pretending to use the new Gus as a mirror. Then he sucked in his gut, tightened his belt, and headed out the door, thermos in hand.

So the development people didn't like Gus. Well, they could join the club. No one likes the sheriff until they need him. The people in the development were no different than anyone else in that regard.

The ranchers used to be kings in this county, and even today many good ranchers made a profit. Gus was driving on the interstate that cut through the heart of the ranching countryside. He was trying hard to follow the direction Ernie had dictated to Lupita. After a short while, Gus passed the property lines and was now into Ernie's ranch land. It would have been easier had Ernie just met him at the front gate of the ranch, but that's not what the note said to do.

The brown fields of grass rolled by the window as Gus searched for a man sitting on his horse. He finally saw him and pulled the truck over to the side of the road. Ernie motioned Gus to come over to a little spot off from the roadside, down to where Ernie's wooden property fence, topped with barbed wire, ran through the tall brown grass. No doubt some cattle thieves had cut through the fence at that location.

Gus headed out of the truck to meet Ernie but was temporarily distracted by another sight. There was a billboard garishly staring down on the interstate a thousand feet farther down the road. On the billboard was Lance Daniels's shining face glaring down. Gus thought, really, they can afford billboard signs? No one drove these back-road interstates but truckers and the local ranchers. Advertising here sure seemed like a stupid place to spend your money (if you had money to spend on billboards, which Gus didn't). In a bad mood, Gus walked into the tall grass to meet up with Ernie.

"Gus, it's over here. They came in the night and cut my fence! I guess after that they just plopped it over the wooden rails," shouted Ernie from his horse.

"Yeah, yeah. When the hell did they put up that damn billboard?"

"Huh? I don't know, few days ago, I guess. I didn't even know you were retiring." Ernie moved the horse closer to Gus's spot by the rails of the fence.

Gus waved his cowboy hat in the air in frustration. "I ain't retiring, Ernie, if I can help it. All you have to do is vote for me and not him. It seems pretty simple, doesn't it? Now can we get off the subject, as I'm sorry I brought it up? Tell me where exactly this unpleasant problem is."

Gus started moved around in the tall grass, looking for signs of it being matted down by cattle. He could see the outline of the razor wire through the grass and a clear open spot where the thieves cut through it. It didn't look like they got many cattle out this way. Not over the still-intact wooden rails of the fence.

Ernie rode over to the opening in the fence. "I figure what happened, Gus, is that they cut the wire and then pushed the body over the rails of the fence. At least I guess they did it that way. A couple of my boys found the body early this morning. I told them to call your office while I rode out here to make sure the animals stayed away from it, so as to preserve the evidence for you. Oh, this is just all too terrible, with you retiring and now

17

this happening! I'll be honest, Gus, I've never seen anything as terrible as this before in my whole life-so young and pretty too."

All this bellyaching over a pretty calf seemed rather pointless to Gus, though not as pointless as the thieves that were trying to steal it in the middle of the night. They were clearly not proper cattle thieves. They were probably just a bunch of young idiots looking for a bit of fun. They likely tore the calf up trying to push it over the razor wire. There were too many dumbasses in this county. What are you going to do with another man's branded cow anyways? Ernie electronically branded his cattle with computer chips in the ears. Young idiots probably wouldn't know that. This whole county was full of stupid kids that grew up into stupid adults. People claimed it was not possible to become educated going to the public schools around here, and the evidence supported that notion in Gus's mind. The only exception maybe was that charter one in the development, but it was exclusive and expensive. Fuck the development people, thought Gus, they would ruin the charm of the town with their exclusionary charter schools and their new sheriff.

Gus's mind stopped wandering and suddenly focused on the problem at hand. He noticed there wasn't any dead cow on his side of the fence.

"Is the body on this side of the fence or your side, Ernie? I thought you said they pushed it over."

"They did push it over to this side."

Well, that answer didn't make any sense. Why would an idiot steal a cow then push the same cow back over razor wire to the place they tried to steal it from? Gus frowned at the prospect of climbing over the fence. If the evidence was on the other side, then, sigh, he would do it. Nothing in this job was easy, thought Gus.

Gus placed his leg on the bottom rail and hoisted himself up. In a quick motion he used his momentum to swing his other leg up and over the top rail, but the motion was too rapid for old Gus and he found he was off balance. He tried too late to shift his weight and judged incorrectly which way to lean to get his balance correct. Down Gus slipped from the top of the fence. He landed in the pasture below with an audible thud. His lower back popped in a dull ache.

Gus was now lying flat on his back in the pasture. And he wasn't alone. Someone was lying right beside him. A rather young blonde woman—rather attractive, thought Gus. She certainly was not a cow, and clearly she shouldn't be here. The woman was dressed in a stretch T-shirt, a pair of tight black shorts, a pair of knee-high socks, and sneakers. Gus blinked his eyes to make sure he hadn't knocked himself silly with the fall. He rolled over to his stomach and crawled over to the young woman for a closer inspection. She couldn't have been more than twenty-five; she was probably younger, and the makeup just made her appear older to Gus. Her hair was nice, long, clean, and gave off a pleasant smell. Her nails were painted bright red. All of this was in her favor, and if her skin wasn't pale and her open eyes lifeless, Gus would have thought she was a pretty good catch for some young man. But now she was very dead and lying with Gus in Ernie's field. She clearly shouldn't be here; she probably shouldn't be dead either, thought Gus.

Gus heard Ernie's voice somewhere over the tall grass. "Did you find her, Sheriff?"

Gus struggled back up to his feet and brushed off evidence of his fall to try to regain a little dignity. As he bent back over to grab the cowboy hat from the ground, the small of his back sent out a pain. He grimaced a little but managed to stand back up and place the hat on his head. He then nodded very slowly at Ernie. He found her, all right, but he wasn't sure what to make of her. A very measured, thoughtful voice in Gus's head said, "Just what you didn't need: an unsolved murder of a pretty blonde girl during election season."

"I found her, Ernie. There's going to be a lot of people here in a little bit, so anything you need to tell me, it is best that you tell it to me right now," warned Gus.

The midday sun was getting to Gus by the time the coroner arrived. Gus remembered the early days when he could count on his coroner, good old Dr. Smith-Wesley. The doctor was always a lot of fun at an investigation scene. He was the type that was quick with a joke—a good Mexican joke if the person looked Hispanic, a lot of Aggie jokes if the person looked Texan. No doubt old Dr. Smith-Wesley would have lightened Gus's mood up today with a few tasteful blonde jokes. It was too bad that old Dr. Smith-Wesley had gotten cancer and passed away last year.

Now the county had Dr. Chloe Armstrong. There wasn't much technically wrong with Chloe. She just didn't have that good-old-boy spirit that lightened up the presence of death. She was always too official for Gus's taste. In the old days you could arrest a man and beat a confession out of him based on a few minutes of Dr. Smith-Wesley looking at a body. The forensic evidence in the end didn't always come back from the lab and point to the person's guilt, but Dr. Smith-Wesley never got an innocent man beaten up. No, it was just that a few weren't guilty of that particular crime.

But this Chloe was different. She always needed all the time she could get. She had all kinds of tests Gus and Dr. Smith-Wesley never heard of. She had all kind of rules for collecting evidence that didn't seem all that important before. Worst of all, she didn't like jokes of any kind. Dead bodies were usually stiff enough; Gus didn't need a stiff coroner too.

While Chloe did the real work on the investigation scene, Gus amused himself playing with the yellow caution tape and trying to square off the area. Before they'd all showed up he'd had plenty of time for a good look around for anything obvious, but nothing stuck out. The crime scene consisted of a body, a cut fence, and a few boot tracks that Ernie said came from when his boys found her. It was actually funny how clean the area was, considering it was a pasture. Maybe they'd get lucky and last night a witness drove by while it was happening, but that seemed at best a slim hope. Once it got in the papers he'd know for sure, because everyone in town would be talking about it. Boys killing boys over drugs hardly caused a stir these days, but a pretty blonde girl from parts unknown still did. And the wrong people would probably blame Gus for letting it happen. Why couldn't she have gone and got herself killed after the election? One thing Gus had learned being sheriff is that people did not conveniently die according to your schedule.

Gus was biding his time with fake busywork until he judged enough time had lapsed and the county investigation team had finished their search of the area. This was an unusual case for this county. The county generally had two kinds of suspicious deaths. There was the drunk or high good-old boy that shoots a relative or coworker in anger and basically confesses to it or, easier yet, up and shoots himself right on the spot. The other kind was the occasional death among the border drug runners. Usually those guys were careful to leave no clues and were nice enough to kill someone no one cared about. They also tend to place the bodies out in the wasteland where people don't bother to look. Neither of those kinds of deaths were all that mysterious. In this case someone at least panicked and stashed the body in a way so as to leave not much to tell Gus what happened. When he judged there wasn't much more that needed yellow tape, he moseyed back over to the fence. He put his two elbows on the top rail and peered down at the coroner, still busy examining the body.

"Chloe, how about it? Any possibility you can tell me anything useful about this dead girl yet?"

Chloe replied without bothering to stop what she was doing. "Well, for one thing she isn't a girl, she's a young woman. For another thing this young woman's death is very suspicious. Lastly, my name is Dr. Armstrong. We are business associates, and I think I deserve the same respect as any other professional here."

"I wasn't aware you respected any other professional here. There is no need for all that sass, little lady. We are all the good guys, remember? Save your sass for the state boys if they show up. I figured it was a suspicious death, as gir—young women don't normally go walking for fun in cow pastures and drop dead of natural causes on a daily basis. You understand, it is important to old Sheriff Gus to get ahead of this situation, so if you've got more information to give, please give it. This situation looks like one of those real, honest-to-god mysteries. I need to know if it was murder for sure and how exactly this gir—young woman died. So do you have any clues along that line that will help me?"

Chloe now stood up and faced Gus over the fence. "I'm taller than you, Gus, so don't ever call me little lady. You know darn well I can't tell you anything official until I get her back and do a full examination. It looks like her neck was broken, but I can't be sure that was the cause of death. You'll have my official report in a few days, weeks, or months. I usually have to wait on the city for the toxicology laboratory reports before I'm a hundred percent sure. But I think you can probably start on the hunch she didn't do this to herself."

Gus straightened up, stood tall by the fence, and frowned as Chloe still looked down on him. "I was taller than you when I was your age. It's this darn job, you know. It weighs on you over the years. There's probably an official doctor name for it."

"It's called aging, Gus, and it isn't just reserved for sheriffs," replied Chloe.

"Well, do this old man a little more service and feel free to do a little more speculating about our friend the body lying right there."

Chloe shrugged. "Well, as you probably noticed, there are a lot of footprints around the body here…"

"Those are from Ernie's boys when they found her. By the way, Ernie officially found her, but unofficially it was his boys. Anyways, I'm pretty sure those are from them, as none of them were also on this side of the fence. Those are male boots for sure, and they lead up back to the main horse path. You see, I did some investigation before you showed up, and I'm willing to share my information."

It was now Chloe's turn to frown. "You plan to lie in the official record about who found the body? Well, I can't. I'm saying I found the tracks and I'll leave it up to you to tell people how they got there. The criminal investigation crew already took pictures of them. Although I have to agree with you that Ernie's boys are in the clear. They're too lazy to cut their own fence, because they know they'd be the ones that have to fix it. More to the point, she wouldn't date one of them any day on Earth."

Gus adjusted his cowboy hat on his head and rubbed his temples. "She looks kind of fancy with her nails and hair, but all she's got on is a T-shirt and a pair of shorts. That ain't exactly a high-class chick in my book. You are suggesting someone wasn't dating her, but renting her an hour at a time?"

Chloe leaned on the fence even closer to Gus and spoke firmly. "My first guess was that we were looking at a first-class prostitute. Her well-done breast implants and that nose job, might indicate that. However the little tattoo on the small of her neck under the hair changed my mind. I'm pretty sure it's the mascot of the state school up in the city. It is what you call these days a social trend. She's wearing a shirt that will run you maybe one hundred to a hundred and fifty dollars, and those designer yoga shorts might run a young woman twice that. A lot of rich party girls from California go to that particular school. I'd say she was one of them. Her age, her clothes, and her tattoo all fit the college-student scenario. It's just a guess on my part, but it's my best guess until I can get her back and do a full official report. Is that enough to help you, or would you like me to find the person that dumped her here too?"

Gus smiled back at her. "Sorry for the negative thoughts. You did old Dr. Smith-Wesley proud with that speculating. By the way do you think she's been…you know."

Chloe shrugged. "Raped? I certainly won't know that for a while yet. I'll be leaving you now; here comes the spokesman for the fourth estate. I'll let you run along and play while I finish doing the real investigation work."

Oh crap, thought Gus. Just what he didn't need at this moment: a pretty blonde girl, dead from an unknown cause-and possibly a sex maniac on the loose-splashed all over the county news. Gus needed to handle how the press covered this story, or he'd be blamed for sure. Everything this morning was sucking the air was out of his campaign. He didn't need another reason for people to notice him not doing the job to their satisfaction.

Gus moved away from the fence toward Deputy Drew's patrol car, which had just pulled up with Marty Laird riding shotgun. Marty Laird was most of the county press. At least the part that mattered, as most of the newspaper was put together from recycled national wire-service stories. Marty was the only person that covered the local news. The county gazette was the longest-running paper in the area. Most of the people in the county read it, at least of those who read the news. Of course, the young people got their news on the Internet. They weren't interested in the hick town news anymore; they all wanted to know what was going on in the big cities on the coasts. As far as Gus could figure out, Marty made up for declining sales with more sensational local news. Gus had to admit, the paper was getting more interesting to read, even if it contained less actual news. But Gus wasn't about to help Marty use this suspicious death to boost circulation. He scrambled quickly now up to the side of the road to intercept Marty before he got too much news from anyone else.

Deputy Drew spoke first. "Sheriff, I bumped into Marty at the station. He was wondering what all the news on the police band was about, so I told him I could drive him up here and check it out. I did good, huh, boss?"

"Thank you, Deputy. There is absolutely no one I'd rather see at this criminal investigation scene than a member of the press. I am sure I've told you this before, but I'll gladly tell you again, for the official public record, that you clearly are a credit to your father. Now do me a favor and take this roll of yellow tape and go yellow tape anything you think might look suspicious. Don't worry about wasting it either. Use it freely, boy; that's one of the perks of the job." Gus handed the yellow police tape to the deputy and came around the squad car to intercept Marty.

Marty was used to ignoring any negative comments about him moved over to shake Gus's hand. "Why, if it isn't Sheriff Gus in the flesh, and might I add what a pleasure it is to see you again. I heard there's a dead body here. You couldn't by chance let me get a few photographs? I promise I won't tamper with the evidence."

"Marty, you know I'd love to let you do that, but think of the horror of the next of kin finding out their love one was dead on your front page. Right now all I can say is we got a Jane Doe of approximately twenty to twenty-five. I promise you, once we identify the body and notify the next of kin, you will be my very next call."

"Come on, Gus, there aren't that many people in this county. If you don't know her, it means the body is pretty mangled, or better yet she's an out-of-towner. Which is it, Gus? The public has a right to buy my paper and find out!"

"She doesn't appear to be a local, but you never know for sure until we identify her. She could be from the development. There are a lot of new people in there, but like I've said, we are still trying to identify her. I promise as soon as I know who she is, right after her next of kin, it's you I will tell." Gus was starting to run out of ways to phrase that last point.

"Sex maniac?" asked Marty hopefully.

Gus put his hand on Marty's shoulder. "I sure as hell don't want you saying there are crazy sex maniacs running around during my reelection campaign unless it is accurate, and maybe not even then. It might cause a public panic. You're the press. You're supposed to be neutral on politics, so make sure you help me and society out and don't get too sensational without clear facts. You can trust me to get you the information before the city paper up north if you help things stay calm for right now. Do you know what I mean? Come on, Marty. Help me help you out, and keep things in perspective."

"Aw, Gus, you know me. I have always been neutral in your direction when it comes to elections. But between you and me, someone is mailing the paper some pretty nasty editorials about you. I've resisted the temptation to print them. Might I add that they come with some pretty big checks?"

"But you can't be bribed, right, Marty?"

"Of course not, but the paper at times does need donations. A free press ain't totally free, and I'm all for staying as neutral as I can afford to."

"Well, try to stay neutral a little longer, and I'll get you some stuff on this case, I promise."

"You can start getting it to me anytime…" said Marty, pen and pad in hand.

"If you think I'm holding out on you right now, then you're wrong. There is not much info about who did it, who it was done to, or what exactly was done. For that we got to wait for the forensics reports to come out."

Marty stopped writing in his pad. "I hate to break it to you, Gus, but a dead pretty blonde girl that might possibly be dead from homicide isn't exactly going to be easy to present in a neutral way. People love hearing about beautiful people, particularly if something bad happens to them. They are going to soak this story up, overreact, and panic no matter how nicely I put it. You better hope she fell off her horse or something boring like that. Otherwise people will be writing in and looking at their neighbors as if they're sex maniacs. Oh, and the first people they are going to blame is Ernie, then his boys, and finally you."

Gus shook his head to the negative. "Do me a favor, and write that Ernie and his crew are not suspects at present. Another thing: as long as you are still being all neutral and stuff towards me, can you find out who is supplying Lance Daniels with all his money? I mean, editorial bribes, that billboard..." Gus lifted his hat in the direction of the billboard to high-light it to Marty. "That kind of advertising stuff has to take real money. I smell a story in that billboard, don't you, Marty?"

Marty looked at the billboard. "You know, Gus, you're not as dumb as the barrel boys think. I hadn't really thought of that, but that is an actual story. I'll tell you what, if you get more information on this murder and get it to me first, then if I find something on Daniels I'll get the news to you first. It will all be nice and neutral between the both of us."

"Nice and neutral, Marty; I like that. Come on, I'll give you a lift back to town. I have to start the work of finding out who she was. This whole thing is unfortunately bound to be interesting."

"Pretty blonde dead girls are always interesting, Gus." Marty snapped a photo of Gus in his cowboy hat, awkwardly standing next to the sher-iff truck and surrounded by yellow tape. A stock photo of a pretty dead blonde girl next to a photograph of a bumbling old sheriff was all Marty needed for the perfect beginning of a viral Internet story.

CHAPTER 2

It was a new morning, but Gus was sitting back at his old desk looking over a manila folder that contained all the information from the case. He didn't have much. He was filling out official forms when he noticed an annoying shadow that kept creeping over the forms. Then he remembered he was wearing the stupid hat. He took it off and threw it into the inbox. The office door slammed in the distance. Probably Deputy Drew back from sleeping another one off and ready to start a new day.

There was a little red envelope sitting in the inbox. Gus slipped the envelope out from under the hat. The envelope was address to Sheriff Gus. There was no return address on it. Only one person sent little red envelopes to Gus. Andrew Murray hired coyotes to bring cheap southern labor to work his meat packing plant. Occasionally one of the untrained illegals lost a limb or an eye in an industrial accident. Injuries could attract the attention of ICE. The envelope was a friendly reminder to make sure they wouldn't. Gus tore it open. He slid the generous check out of the envelope. He slid the check into his front pocket.

He looked at the crime scene photographs of the dead girl. She was really a young woman, but to Gus people that age were still just boys and girls in grown-up bodies. He remembered his daughter at that age. She thought she knew everything, no matter how many times Gus tried to tell her she didn't. Just like a little girl. Now, as far as Gus could tell, his daughter did know everything, or was at least smart enough to be smarter than him. Gus had sent his only child away to California for college seven years ago and she hadn't been back since. However he did get a monthly love letter from her in the form of her college loan bill. Money lenders are better at timely correspondence than fathers or daughters.

The case wasn't officially a homicide yet, but everyone knew it would be. By the end of last night, Gus had it figured down to a traveling sex maniac. A sex maniac that was at least five states away now. That would be best for everyone in the county. They could call in the FBI, and before long everyone would forget about it. Of course, if it was a local and Gus solved it…well, that would help his reelection chances.

Gus looked over at the stupid sign Terrance left in his office. Times had changed. The big boys of politics were no longer in control. But if Gus solved the case, he wouldn't really need the boys anymore. He could ride good publicity to a successful reelection. He'd stick it to old Lance Daniels and his secret money men. He looked over at his inbox with the cowboy hat sitting in it. It was still election season. A sheriff couldn't afford to get caught taking money during the election season. He probably shouldn't take money during any season. Gus wasn't looking to find religion. He was just looking forward to still finding his biweekly paycheck. He never saw himself as an immoral man anyways. All he needed was to show the voter what kind of a morally sound sheriff he could be if he was free from the burdens placed on him by the boys. Morality had its price too, but unfortunately no one bribes you to act morally. He slid Murray's check out of his pocket. He tore the check in half and placed it back into the red envelope. He placed the envelope in the out box. Andrew Murray would just have to learn to hire a few legal workers from now on.

The path seemed easy now. The actors on TV solved a crime like this every week, and they weren't even real detectives. Not that Gus was a real detective either. Gus remembered the time friendly Ned Johnson was shot by his son. He shot him dead with a forty-four in a fit of anger, because he caught his dad smoking his weed. He called up 911 and confessed to it right there in the house while standing next to the body. That was about as close to a murder mystery as Gus had ever solved.

You had to have clues, thought Gus. Gus opened up the manila folder to look at all his clues: blonde, female, tattoo, expensive clothes, and speculation she was possibly from the college up north in the city. That was the end of his clues. They didn't mean much to Gus.

Gus had already called the campus police up north yesterday, but they didn't have any missing persons. He had Lupita fax a tasteful picture of the deceased just in case they suddenly noticed someone was missing. Then he had her send one over to the state police and the FBI. Someone was bound to be missing her eventually. He was hoping to identify her sooner rather than later. She was apparently a very good girl, because she had no fingerprints on file or prior arrests, according to the computer. This helped scratch out even more the idea she was a prostitute. There were always her dental records, but that could take forever and a day. The last resort would be posting a picture of the dead girl in the media and hoping someone called in. He didn't want to do that yet, although it would really get him on Marty's good side. Reading it on the news, or worse, splashed up on TV, seemed a terrible way to find out your daughter was dead. A parent ought not to learn news like that the same time as a bunch of strangers that didn't care at all.

Although, truth be told, Gus agreed with Marty that the strangers would all care a lot. Strangers cared and loved news about missing young blonde girls who were very pretty and possibly rich, particularly if they died at the hands of a sex maniac. There officially wasn't a sex maniac in this case yet, but Gus thought it was a matter of time before Chloe found evidence of rape. What else could it be? Already they had locals calling in suspicious-person reports.

Well, if she was local and a good girl, then the high schools would remember her. Gus decided to head out to the local high schools and see if anyone could identify a photograph of her. He tried the rural ones first but didn't have any luck there. He wasn't shocked, as he knew she was unlikely to be from this county.

He went over to the fancy new charter high school built in the development. The principal there was a rude prick of a bastard. Gus had to wait an hour for five minutes of the guy's time. Then the principal refused to say a word to Gus until he removed his stupid cowboy hat indoors. It had something to do with manners. According to the principal, good manners somehow identified dead victims faster. In this case, hat on or off, it didn't seem to matter, as the principal had never seen the victim before. It had only taken seconds once the principal bothered to look.

Gus headed back to the sheriff's office. He couldn't think of anything else productive to do. His hopes now fell on his world-class and much brighter coroner finding out who the victim was from the magic of those new devices she loved.

Gus was in luck when he returned to the office. Lupita was waiting for him with news that one might have viewed as good.

"Sheriff, the campus police called you back. They said the picture looks like one of three students someone just reported to them as possibly missing."

"Three! I only got one dead body. I sure hope this doesn't mean I got two more to find. Who reported her missing?"

"Nigel Laurence. Apparently he was the young woman's resident advisor at the college."

"And the dead girl's name is?"

"They think it is Cherry Colston. She was a student of the college. The other missing girls were Pam Martin and Michelle Hardy. I guess I should say *are*, as we don't know if they're dead too. But with you on the case, I might guess that they'll be dead before you ever find them."

"Thanks for the confidence. Did you ask them how long they've been missing? Not officially missing, but when they unofficially were last seen."

"Saturday night is what the campus police told me. I wrote everything down like a good detective," said Lupita, holding up a sticky note with all her information scribbled down in shorthand on it.

"Saturday was a long time ago. Nigel sure took his sweet-ass time reporting these girls' disappearance. You did a good job questioning, Lupita. You're a better detective than I am."

"We all know that already, and thank goodness. Someone will need to train the new guy. You want me to call the campus police up so you can officially speak to them?" asked Lupita.

Gus rubbed his left temple and thought it over. "Nah. I think I owe the college campus a personal visit. You go ahead and get them to send down pictures of the two other missing girls. We might as well send the deputies around town looking for them. You never know where a pretty young girl might turn up in this county these days."

"I was already in the process of doing that. Also I am looking through the database for sex maniacs that may have come to the area."

"Yeah, that's a good idea too. Glad one of us has them. I tell you what, you keep doing useful stuff here, and I'll drive up north to the city and drag down their investigation."

"How idiots ever become sheriff I will never know," replied Lupita.

"The people vote us into office," pointed out Gus, and then he tipped his hat to her and was off to the city.

Gus didn't like places of higher learning. While his dad had been pro education, Gus's friends, teachers, and pastor had all advised him to be against it. As far as Gus could tell, college was an excuse for people to extend their childhood four to ten years before entering the reality of actual adulthood. The only difference between college and preschool was the amount of drinking and sex the student body could legally participate in.

The natural thing would be to talk to the campus police right away. Gus had driven instead to the three girls' dormitory. Apparently they had been missing five days, and it just occurred to the people in charge of watching these grown children that there might be a problem. Gus wanted to hear the reason for the delay. In Gus's mind, boys that delayed reporting of missing girls were suspicious.

According to the campus police, the body was Cherry Colston, formerly of the city of Los Angeles. Thanks to Lupita, the manila folder was updated, and it told Gus that Cherry had been an heiress to a rather nice fortune. Her parents had sent her to college to get an education, but according to the rumor mill young women went to this particular school for other reasons. It was a notorious party school, a fantasy land where the rich and beautiful spent their early twenties drunk or stoned. The smart ones got their marriage degrees and a road to a happy future of divorce settlements, tennis pros, and plastic surgery. In Gus's mind, Los Angeles was like some fantastic scum pit that ought to keep its residents away from his county. Whatever realities of life Cherry had learned at this college, it was only the short crash course at the end that was relevant to people like Gus.

Gus pulled the official sheriff truck into a parking spot in front of the dormitory. A small sign in front read Pleasant Hall. Pleasant was the last word one would use to describe the building. It looked like any other shabby concrete quick-build from the nineteen seventies era, back when orange, yellow, and brown were considered a suitable color palette combination.

A man in a small three-wheeled cart pulled up behind Gus. He was shouting something at Gus. He had a made-to-order uniform on that gave him a false air of mythical authority. Gus couldn't hear him, so he rolled down the window.

"I'm afraid, sir, that you can't park there. Visitors must park at the designated visitor parking at the main hall only."

"See the markings on my truck? They say I can park here."

"Look, mister, I respect that you're law enforcement and all that, but a visitor is a visitor. I don't make the rules. My job is only to enforce them. I know it's stupid, but a visitor is a visitor."

"Look, I'm on official sheriff business and I'm parking here," replied Gus in a louder voice.

"I don't see your lights on."

Gus reached over and flipped the lights on for the truck. "Do you want the sirens too?"

"No, that's fine. You're now, according to the official campus rules, here on official business, so I can let you park there without a ticket. Rules are rules, you know." The man pulled his head back into the three-wheeled cart and puttered down the parking lot, looking for more potential revenue for the school.

"Leeches," said Gus out loud. There was no one around to hear it, but it made him feel better just the same.

Gus went up to the main door of the hall, but it was locked. Despite the college being located in one of the better parts of the city, the dorm was still secured to the teeth. There was an electronic-swipe lock pad on the door, bars on all the low-lying windows, and a security camera. It was a pretty sound security system, thought Gus. It was all just for show, of course. It existed so when all the bill-paying moms and dads visited they would know their little angels would be safe and sound. Yeah, safe from the outside world, but too bad the vast majority of the crimes on campus were committed by all those sweet little angels. Everyone imagined masked men coming onto campus and sweeping up their little darling. In the meantime their little darling was getting dumped in Ernie's field, and probably because some other little darling beat her and raped her.

A pretty young woman in a short skirt came up to the door and waved her proximity card by the lock. The door made a popping sound and she opened it. She smiled politely to Gus and waved him through. Before he could pass inside, two dirty-looking boys walked out, brushing up against Gus in the process. They smelled like perfume, and Gus made a face. The young woman holding the door apologized to Gus for the rudeness of the boys. She noticed Gus's funny face and told him she disliked body spray too; the boys thought it covered for a lack of a shower, but it didn't. They shared a short laugh together, and then he went into the college dormitory.

His new friend made her way into the dormitory proper, thus leaving Gus alone in a small entrance annex with a wall lined with mailboxes. There were two doors on each side of the mailboxes, one marked Cleaning Supplies and the other Resident Advisor. Gus knocked on the second door. No one answered. Gus tried the lock. The door was open, so Gus helped himself inside. A young guy was sitting on a couch, typing madly into a flat-screened widget. Gus, now standing in the open doorway, knocked on the door loudly. The young man did nothing but type into his little gadget.

"Hello, this is Sheriff Gus here to ask a few questions, so could you be so kind as to tell the resident advisor that I'm here?"

"Jesus Christ, man, can't you fucking see I'm busy?" The young man looked up to notice Gus had already helped himself inside the office. "This is a private office! Not just anyone can barge in here!"

"See this little badge? It says I can. Now once again, I'd like to ask a few questions. It won't take long, and you can get back to whatever it is you were doing. Trust me, the one thing I don't care about is what you were doing." Gus walked fully into the office and let the door close behind him.

"Just like the fucking Man to force his way in! I read about what you people did in Egypt, Boston, Syria, and Libya. The Man is the same everywhere. So you are here to give me the third degree too?"

"Are you Nigel Laurence?" asked Gus, hoping the answer was no.

"I don't have to tell you anything. I read the Internet, so I know my rights. I read what happened to those prisoners over in the Middle East. Josh Hansen posted all the photos. The American cowards we call the free press wouldn't show what the Man did over there, but Hansen has the guts to. He shows you every gory detail and in high definition quality if you pay for the premium package! I saw the corruption in the Swiss police, the Russian banks, and the Malaysian slave-labor camps. The Internet is the only place the truth actually exists. It is the only place people like you haven't stolen the truth, locked it up, and thrown away all the keys. Well, you can try, but you can't control the truth. The truth always escapes—like Josh Hansen famously said before he escaped and went into hiding. But his website lives on, and everyone reads it. It's the most popular website on campus."

He stood up from the couch and came closer to Gus. He looked angry and Gus couldn't understand why. It apparently had something to do with whatever the conversation was about. Gus wished he knew what the conversation was about. Then he thought better of it and was glad he didn't.

The young man ranted on. "Well, you can't shut Josh Hansen up and you can't shut me up! Go ahead and beat me, torture me—you won't get a word out of me, you fucking pig. Give me a good squeal, piggy, and go on and hit me. I know how you fascists work, so hit me, you little pig. I will never talk!"

This was clearly the type of young man you wanted in charge of a dorm filled with young woman. Gus looked around the room. They were pretty alone. Gus punched the raving lunatic square in the jaw. The force knocked the young man back on his rear end onto the couch. The young man was dazed and surprised Gus had actually hit him like he had asked. When the young man finally made it back to his feet, Gus hit him with a left. The young man sailed back into the couch. This time he landed on his electronic device, which made a crunching sound.

"Would you care for me to hit you more? I generally don't do requests, but on the other hand I don't like to disappoint people, so if you care for more of a beating, please just go ahead and ask me," said Gus in a rather tired manner.

"You can't do that to me," replied the young man, sounding like he might break into tears at any moment. The young man started dabbing his now heavily bleeding nose with his shirt tails.

"I'm sorry, I was confused. You did ask me to hit you, didn't you? Let me give you a word of wisdom that you don't get in a college lecture: don't ask for a beating if you don't want one." Gus took out a photograph of Cherry from his shirt pocket. He placed it on the young man's lap. "Are you the one that reported this young woman missing? Try not to bleed on that; it's my only copy."

"Yeah, I'm Nigel," said the young man in a rather nasal tone.

"Well, tell me about the missing girl, if you would."

"Not much to tell. Michelle Hardy's roommate came down yesterday night and said she hadn't seen here roommate since Saturday. She was starting to get worried, so I went and told the campus police they were missing. College kids come and go all the time. I don't see the big deal."

"So you don't know where they went?" asked Gus.

"Look, I'm a resident advisor not a freaking nurse maid. I open doors for drunken kids too wasted to do it themselves. I find lost laundry cards, I make change for the vending machines, and I rent out vacuums. Occasionally I tell them to turn down the music and try to prevent too much under-age drinking. But what the fuck, man, it isn't like I got any real authority. These are grown adults. If they do stupid shit now and then, there isn't much I can do."

Gus felt sort of bad now for hitting the nutty kid. Gus knew how he felt. Grown adults generally should know better, but they rarely did. Even with a badge people tended to ignore you and go off and do stupid shit right in front of your face—like tell a sheriff to beat you for no good reason.

"Do you think this roommate of Michelle might be able to tell me a little more information?" asked Gus.

"I figure she might. Mandy Henderson is her name. Her room is on the third floor. It's room three hundred thirteen."

"Thanks." Gus took his photo back from Nigel and put it back in his pocket. "Sorry for hitting you. No hard feelings? But when I see a man go hysterical, I got to calm him down."

"Yeah, I'm sorry too. I get worked up when I read Josh Hansen's website. The revolution is coming, man. It's not your fault that when it does come, the whole old world order will fall down. Total information awareness is coming. No more secrets, just the truth that the authorities don't want the people to know. Then people like you will be over. It's the truth. Nothing you or I can do to stop it."

"I guess," said Gus. Gus left the kid to bleed on his own and headed out to find the roommate.

College was a strange place. It was filled with fired-up, candy-ass momma's boys that wanted revolution but wouldn't ever sign up for any armed service to fight to see it happen. If college taught you that little handheld widgets that surfed the Internet were going to overthrow the world, then Gus wasn't buying it. No small wonder these kids ended up dead in Ernie's field. Gus bet they didn't talk about the drinking, the sex, and the dead girls in the college brochure. "Come to our school, where the RAs are too busy in fantasy land to babysit your little not-so-darling…"

Gus rode the elevator up to the dorm rooms. The elevator smelled like puke. The floor was dirty and the buttons were stained. For the price these kids' parents were paying, you'd think the school would at least try to pretend it was an idyllic place.

The elevator stopped off on the third floor, which was vastly nicer than the elevator. It was cleaner and smelled more like flowers and less like puke. This was clearly the ladies' floor.

Gus knocked on the door to room three hundred thirteen. A rather young attractive girl answered the door in a red and black checkered shirt half opened and revealing what looked to Gus like a white bra underneath. Her lower half was even less covered, just a pair of white panties. Maybe college life wasn't all bad, thought Gus.

"Hello, miss. I'm Sheriff Gus, and I'm looking for a woman by the name of Mandy Henderson. Do you know where I might find her?" asked Gus, trying hard not to look directly at her.

"Oh, I'm Mandy. Are you here about my missing roommate?"

"Yes, ma'am, you can, uh…finish dressing. The questions aren't that urgent. I can wait out here in the hall until you are ready."

"Oh, I'm dressed. I was just about ready to head over to class."

"I don't want you to take any offense, but that doesn't look like appropriate attire for doing schoolwork."

"Oh, this is normal around here. Don't you know it's practically a desert out there? I'll throw a skirt on just before heading outside. Trust me, I'd have to wear a lot less than a bikini to get noticed in a school like this."

"Down south we hear stories about you kids up here in college, but I always thought they were a little exaggerated."

"Of, Sheriff, I'm sure you don't know half the stuff we do! I'm here from down south, on a volleyball scholarship, so I've got to keep my grades up or else no education for me. But the rich kids like my roommate party twenty-four seven. That's the last time I saw her, in fact. She, Cherry, and Pam were all heading out to party."

"Do you know where they were going?"

"Like I told the campus police, they were all heading out with someone they met at Zak Silva's big party Friday night. You know all about the river walk district, right?"

"I know there are a lot of nice places up here next to the river," answered Gus.

"Well, duh, right? A lot of the big shots own condos and such down on the river area. The place has a lot of bars and nightclubs as well, if you're into that thing. The places are owned mostly by rich guys from out of town. Some married, some not. It doesn't really matter, as everyone knows you buy a place there to see people and to be seen. The rich come in on the weekends and throw parties. They love us college kids—we're a top-ten party school, after all."

"Well, Zak is a big-time Hollywood producer. He generally has a few stars at his place and an open bar. Cherry's from LA, you know. Her dad knows Zak, but that's not necessarily why she always gets an invite. What can I say, the college girls here got their reputations, generally all bad." She laughed and smiled at Gus.

"So she met someone at the party, and then what?"

"Well, we all like meeting famous people, and apparently he was going to take us all out for some big private weekend thing. A weekend-long bender, you know. You rave for forty-eight hours then puke and try to remember to get to class on Monday morning."

"But you didn't go?"

"Nah, getting pawed at by some fake celebrity all weekend long wasn't my cup of tea. My general opinion is don't find yourself alone with someone too rich or too fake. Those parties are filled with vacuously handsome guys that have shot one bandaid commercial and think they're the next John Travolta. Those types think they can take advantage of anyone, and I'm not the kind of person that likes to be taken advantage of. I go to their parties and drink their booze, but I like to wake up in my own bed… alone."

"But your roommate and her friends weren't like that?"

"Cherry and Pam are from LA. Their families are rolling in it. They were wild before they ever got here. Michelle's from old money out east somewhere. She was all Bible this and praise the lord that the first month here. I think she came here to get away from her parents and to learn how to actually be a person. Some parents never let you have fun, and then suddenly the parents aren't around and boom, the fun begins."

Gus nodded his head. Something certainly went boom. He pulled out the picture of who he believed was Cherry. "This is a picture of Cherry Colston, isn't it?" asked Gus.

"That's her, all right. She looks really fucked up. What's happened to her?"

As far as Gus knew, the campus police hadn't made an official announcement yet, but Gus was willing to start to let the information out. He needed to get what he could from Mandy.

"She was found dead south of here in a field. We don't know where Pam and Michelle are at this moment. You don't know where they are? They didn't perchance tell you they were running off to Mexico or something wild like that?"

"Dead?"

The word seemed to strike Mandy and knock the wind out of her. She wandered back into her room, leaving the door open, and sat down on a small couch. Gus went into the room after her. It was a small room with two beds, sink, and two dressers. The young women had made the room up as best they could to give it a friendly feel. Gus could search the room for clues to where they went, but he figured Mandy did that already. He didn't have all the time in the world, and the room would eventually be searched by the locals. Gus's motto was, When something wasn't likely to be promising, it was better to let the less promising on the force do it.

Gus waited a bit for Mandy to recover, then he asked, "Your friends left here with this person when?"

"Oh, last Friday. It was Tuesday afternoon when I got to thinking something was wrong. I mean, these benders sometimes go long, but this was nearly four days, and they weren't answering their phones. A bunch of us called them. I went to the RA, and he called in the campus police. I figured one of them got pregnant or something dramatic like that. I never figured...Where are Pam and Michelle?"

"We don't know. What can you tell me about this fellow they went off with?"

"Nothing at all really, just that Cherry said he was famous. He was probably a poor man's Justin Bieber that posts his stuff on YouTube and gains fifteen minutes of fame. For what it is worth, Michelle said to me that he was only a rich banker. People exaggerate who they are at those parties. Still Cherry liked to hang around potentially famous people, particularly if they appeared to be rich. She was really beautiful and paid a lot of money to look that way. I always thought it must be nice to be that pretty; I guess it wasn't in the end."

"Don't be so hard on yourself. You look rather nice too." Gus tipped his hat at her.

"Thanks," replied Mandy.

An unconformable feeling came over Gus. It occurred to him that the reporters would eventually talk to Mandy. It wouldn't sound good if they were able to turn a friendly off-hand comment into an attempt at sexual harassment. Gus was going to have to be more careful with his compliments. The media could turn any innocent situation into a potential sensational expose even an off-hand compliment spoken to a half-naked young woman while alone with her in her dorm room. Being accused of hitting a college student was one thing, but being accused of hitting on one was another.

"Just being friendly and trying to cheer you up."

"Oh, I understand. I know you weren't making a pass at me." Mandy now sat in the couch with her one hand under her chin, lost in thought. "Let's see what I can remember for you. They were all packed with overnight bags that they carried down to the car. He didn't come inside, so I never got a good look at him. He phoned them when he arrived, and they headed down to meet him. I didn't even hear his voice, I'm afraid. I really wish I knew more," said Mandy, looking worried.

Gus went over to the window. It had a nice view down into the parking lot. He could see the lights on his truck flashing and circling as they drained his battery for no good reason.

"Did you look out the window? I know people do sometimes get a little curious and peek out windows to see who their friends are meeting."

"Well, of course I did, Sheriff. I don't mind admitting that. Oh, that's it! I saw his car! He had a limited-edition blue Mercedes. It was really a nice machine too. Oh, and there was another car! A black car that was not as nice that followed the blue car. I think they were together, but they really didn't belong together. I remember thinking at the time it might be for some sort of security detail. Famous people do have security, but then again it could have been just another partygoer. As a matter of fact, they could have been just two cars parked next to each other leaving at the same time by coincidence."

"So you can't be sure about a second car?" asked Gus.

"Wasn't obviously with them for sure, but it did follow them off campus and made a turn right out of the gate just like they did. I mean, it could be a coincidence, right? But I did notice it all the same. Does everyone know about her being dead?"

"No, not yet. I believe we are waiting to get a more positive identification, but it will be out before day's end. I hope I can trust you to keep this information to yourself until it is made official. I know it isn't exactly nice news. The press will be informed, and then they'll be all over this place. It is wise not to tell anyone the news yet, as the press won't mind blurting it out before its proper time, if you know what I mean."

"I do, and trust me, Sheriff; I never wanted that kind of fame," said Mandy.

"Some people do, you know. We downstate people are made of better stuff. If you think of something else you think is important or even not important, feel free to call." Gus gave her his card.

"Sheriff, where is Michelle? You're holding something back from me, aren't you? If she's dead too, I want to know. I need to know." She looked obviously and honestly worried to Gus.

"I honestly don't know. All I can guess is either she is part of the cause of this trouble or she is also in trouble. Other than that…"

Mandy shook her head violently. "The three of them are party girls, not thugs. They caused a lot of trouble maybe for marriages and bank accounts but not to each other. We aren't like that, and we are all really close friends."

"No, doesn't sound right to me either. Do me a favor and find some friends to be around the rest of the day. By nighttime the news will be out."

Gus put his hand on her shoulder and tried to look comforting. She wasn't much comforted. Gus was never much good at dealing with his own daughter and thus didn't really expect he'd be able to offer much fatherly comfort.

Gus headed out of the dormitory. Circling outside was a little three-wheeled cart with a different man than before eyeing his truck. Those parking patrols were a greedy lot, so they might have a record of every strange car that ever came through here. It was a possibility. Gus would have to check that up with campus police, but not yet. Gus had received one more not exactly hot lead he wanted to check out first.

Gus started up the truck. He was in a hurry to make his next visit before the world knew what had officially happened.

The residences of the river district were big, new, and mostly empty. The weekend wasn't here yet, and most of the occupants were either at work or out of town. They were called unofficially "McMansions," but that was only by the people that couldn't afford them. Gus was certainly one of them, but he didn't pretend to hate the houses. They were too new and shiny for Gus to hate. Some people were just lucky in life and some people weren't, and to Gus this appeared to be the land of good fortune.

The best and most expensive homes in the district lined the river bank so that the backs of each home opened up onto the river. Those lucky people each had their own private docks, with a mandatory jet ski and power boat tied up. You could envy these people all you want, but secretly you would have to admit it sounded like a fun life, thought Gus.

Gus spied the number he was searching for, a nice place right on the water line. Gus pulled the truck into the driveway and went up to question the occupant. When he rang the doorbell, a faint chime rang off on the other side of the door, trilling a nice little classical tune that Gus never heard before but that was probably famous and old. The door was popped open by another very pretty, young, fair-haired girl in a yellow bikini bottom and a white print shirt. A person could sure enjoy city life given how a door was generally answered up here, thought Gus.

"Well, hello there, young lady. I'm good old Sheriff Gus, and I'm here to talk to a Mr. Zak Silva. I sure hope you don't mind if I just come inside and see him?" said Gus in as official a voice as possible.

"Boring! Old man is detoxing out on the back porch," answered the girl, rolling her eyes and pouting her face. She pushed the door open wide and gave the look of someone terribly disappointed to see the door had only brought an old fat man. Gus took this as an invitation to come in.

The first room in the house was a large living room filled with expensive furniture in which sat two more rather attractive young girls in bathing suits. They all looked a few years short of college. They were far too interested in themselves to make much notice of Gus, and the three of them moved about on the furniture, gathering the bathing paraphernalia that was scattered about. Gus looked over at the fair-haired girl who had greeted him, but she wasn't paying him any mind. At a certain age, collecting towels and flip-flops with your friends was vastly more important than old law-enforcement officers.

"You girls heading out somewhere?" asked Gus, breaking the awkward silence.

One of the girls turned to finally acknowledge him. "Yeah, mister, we're all about to head out for the swimming pools, so what of it?"

"The river is just out back if you want to go swimming," pointed out Gus.

A girl wearing sunglasses flipped them up so Gus could see her eyes and then tossed a towel over her shoulder. She put her hands to her hips in as sassy a posture as she could make. "Sure, but who wants to swim? Particularly in a river—talk totally gross. Losers swim and we're not losers. The point of swimming pools is to get seen. Class, duh!"

"'Socialize,'" shouted out the fair-haired girl, making air quotes.

The three girls then turned to each other to share a giggle at what Gus was pretty sure was his expense. Gus never claimed to be hip to the younger generation. His generation did swim in the aqueducts that led down from the river as they piped their way south through his county. In his day a kid was lucky to be able to get cool on a hot day.

The girls by now were done packing up their things and had in place three pairs of identical designer sunglasses on their faces to match their three nearly identical sets of clothes. The three nearly identical young manikins then went out the front door, completely immune to Gus's presence.

Kids were all kind of nice and self-absorbed in an unassuming way at that age. Coming from money had an insulating effect on you as well, no doubt. Gus remembered his daughter at that age. She wanted and needed to look like everyone else and complained bitterly to Gus when he offered up excuses as to why a certain shirt was too expensive for their family. Now that she was older she was smart enough not to ask for money. Indeed she could go months between speaking to him at all.

These three probably grew up in a world where they were treated as untouchable. They had private schools, private lessons, and play dates with their own kind of friends. Sure they were taught to watch out for strangers, but someone that was supposed to be safe, like Sheriff Gus, well they were in a perfect position to do a young kid like that harm. These young adults never understood that no one is untouchable. Gus knew one thing for sure: no poor Mexican living in the county down south would have left Gus alone in their house. They knew what people like Sheriff Gus could do alone in a house. Gus shared a private laugh with himself, thinking that those young girls probably thought those Mexicans were just a bunch of idiots. Well, had Zak been an actual murder suspect, all this would matter, but as far as Gus could tell, he wasn't. So Gus skipped tearing the house apart and found his way to the back porch.

The back of the house had a large sun deck with adjoining stairs that led down to a dock. Gus stepped out of the sliding glass door onto the deck where a man in perhaps his early fifties was lying in a sun chair. His hair was jet black and obviously dyed. The hair was matted back and held in place with gel. The man was wearing Bermuda shorts and a casual Hawaiian shirt. The clothes had money to them, and so did the sunglasses he was wearing. On a small glass patio table to the man's right sat two Bloody Marys. It was rather late in the day to just be waking up, thought Gus. Then again, based on stories Mandy told, maybe it was typical behavior for this part of town. These were the kind of people that did a lot of their work after dark.

The guy flipped up his sunglasses upon seeing Gus. He smiled a friendly little smile. "You collecting for something, or did my ex-wife send you?"

Gus was distracted by the sight of the two drinks. It was hot out there on the patio and Gus had been hoping Zak would start the conversation by offering one. Gus was thinking of helping himself without being asked, but he didn't dare try. He figured you couldn't just take a rich man's drink during election season. He would settle for trying to look eager for a drink and hoping Zak would offer one.

"A lot of young pretty girls you have around here," replied Gus.

"My daughter and her friends, officer. She's not in any trouble, is she? I got alimony and child support already."

Gus moved over to the guy in order to stand nearer the drinks on the table. "Oh, no trouble. I'm interested in parties. Your daughter didn't have a party, a real big party, last Friday evening by any chance?"

The guy reached over for his glass and drank a sip of his first Bloody Mary. He didn't appear eager to share. He wiped his lips with his hand. "Fuck no! What kind of father do you think I am? My daughter is way too young for the parties that happen in this part of town, at least I certainly hope she is. If she goes to them in Los Angeles while she's with that bitch of a person she calls her mom …well, then I don't want to hear about it. A dad needs to have certain illusions about his daughter. Caesar's wife and all that, you understand."

Gus nodded his head. He didn't know Caesar or his wife, but he assumed it wasn't important. Gus didn't have any illusions about his own daughter. Heck, when he visited her six months ago she refused to introduce him to any of her bohemian California friends. She always seemed afraid he would do or say something to embarrass her. That helped dispel any illusions he might have.

"There was a party here on Friday night, though, wasn't there?"

"Yeah, but it was my party. I just signed a new client. I had to show off for the young kid, so I threw a little party here to show him why he wanted to work with me. It was nothing big. There's something like that probably every night; every weekend there's probably ten or so big splashes. That's just how it is here. You put on a show so they sign up and do your commercial and promote your product. It all looks fun from the outside perspective, but a lot of it is strictly the dirty business of wooing clients for the entertainment industry," said Zak.

"Were there a lot of young people from the college here that night?"

"Well yeah, the kids always come into these neighborhoods to party. When a bunch of college girls come knocking on your door, you don't exactly turn them away. And it isn't exactly a secret the houses around here throw big parties on the weekends. Everyone is here to party except me; I'm here to woo clients. This is a happening kind of place. If it wasn't, do you think people like me would live here? It's a good atmosphere for client impressing." Zak pulled the celery out of his Bloody Mary and bit into it, looking Gus over to see if he was getting it.

"Was there anyone YouTube famous at the party?"

The only U shaped tube Gus knew about was under his sink. He remembered Mandy using the word and he figured it would mean something more to a hipster like Zak.

"Probably, I guess. Like I said, I had a client over trying to get him into my commercial. Heck, depending on your point of view, nearly everyone around this neighborhood is semi-famous. Some just in their own field, but you know we have real celebrities here, like athletes and singers. About halfway through the party, I took my client upstairs to be private and sign a deal. Who came and went after that I don't know. You'll have to ask around the neighborhood."

Gus took out a picture of Cherry and placed it next to the two drinks on the table. "Have you ever seen this girl before? Like perhaps last Friday night?"

Zak looked a little ill seeing the photograph but managed a white lie rather quickly. "Yeah, I think I know her slightly. I know her father better. We work a lot together in the industry. I can't even remember his daughter's name, though. And as for whom she was with or whom she picked up at my party, well, like I said, you'll have to ask around. I don't even remember for sure if she was at the party. I certainly don't know her from any Internet video or anything like that. I don't know anyone that films Internet porn around here, if that's what all this is about. I produce commercials, not pornography, and not with my friend's daughters. If someone told you a different story, they're lying."

Gus decided to leave him hanging as to what it was all about. He didn't know himself what it was all about. Internet porn? Could be; the missing college women were three young attractive college girls. Still, they didn't sound like the kind of girls that you could lure somewhere to shoot a porn flick. And by all accounts they sure didn't need the money. But you did hear stories of socialites getting famous from "leaked" Internet porn videos. How bad did these girls want to be famous? Gus would write the idea down and put it in the manila folder, but his heart was still figuring on a sex maniac. A sex maniac would have no problem on a Friday night moving through the parties and getting a victim. Everyone was assuming that everyone else was the right kind of person in a place like this.

It would take a lot of work to figure out who was and wasn't at the party, and in the end you'd probably never know everyone's names. Gus would do the smart thing and let the locals waste their time on it. He was getting ready to release the information he had to them, and between the locals and the press, armed with a better picture of Cherry, something might pop. If someone knew something, maybe they'd come forward.

But it was also possible that no one knew anything. A party is a good place to find someone and not be seen. There were literally hundreds of somebodies, so possibly no one would remember one someone from another one. They'd all just be another face in the crowd to each other.

Gus felt finished with Zak. The hot sun and the second glass were both weighing heavily on him. The stories of Zak's parties made it sound like anyone could get a free drink in this house, but Zak's overgenerous manners must have taken a vacation. Gus figured he didn't want to ruin Zak's reputation for generosity so he grabbed the second Bloody Mary Zak hadn't touched yet and drank it down.

"Well, Mr. Silva, thanks for a moment of your time and your drink. If you remember anything more, please call the local police, and they'll get in touch with me."

"You know I will," replied Zak with a wink.

Gus was pretty sure he wouldn't. The man lied about how well he knew the girl, but that didn't mean much regarding her death. Still, the only person likely to hear from Zak was his lawyer. The Zaks of the world didn't want to be on the front page unless it was to sell you something. Tomorrow he'd know this was a murder investigation, and under those circumstances Gus was pretty sure Zak would keep whatever he knew to himself. That was probably true of the whole neighborhood. They would eventually release the information to the papers and TV, but no one semi-famous would risk their neck and fame to say a goddamn thing.

Gus had talked to everyone that he thought could or might have helped him. He had a brief moment where the people up here might have been caught unaware before the news hit. He was hoping to get something or cross someone up, but he didn't feel very successful on that count. And now his head start was about to fade away. The parents had finally been reached and informed about their daughter. An official identification had been made. The TV news in the city would be all over the story. When it was just a no-named girl in the south county, there hadn't been much press. But now that she was a big-city girl, the story would explode.

Gus would have to spend the night up in the city. He had finally made his way to the campus police and confirmed with them who the victim probably was. They were busy dealing with inquires by the city police about the murder and the additional two missing young women. The campus police station was turning into a law-enforcement zoo by the time the state boys finally arrived to snoop around.

A man in a nice, pressed uniform arrived at the campus police station. Gus knew the man well. The man was Brian Hartline, the commissioner of the state police. He didn't look happy to be there. Gus wasn't happy to see him but waved to him anyways.

The commissioner greeted him, "I heard you were in town creating a mess. Have you found a proper student to pin this murder on or are you waiting for the campus police to profile one up for you?"

"I can't just arrest any old person in the middle of an election. The days of pinning and profiling are all in my past. This sheriff's office conducts nothing but perfectly lawful investigations these days."

"Gus, the devil is lawful too; lawful evil. I have a small correction to make to your repentance. You were conducting an investigation. The families of the missing women made calls to lawyers, who made calls to judges, who made calls to me, who made a call to the governor. The governor was on the phone wondering why she wasn't aware of the three missing women earlier and why it wasn't in the city papers! She sent me here to chew out the campus police, the city police, and my own state boys. When I'm done, all of them will be chewing out you. You are now working for me. You are the low man on the totem pole. So everything you learn from now on is typed up nicely and given to my boys. That word comes straight from the governor. Do we have an understanding?"

Gus took the news in stride. It didn't matter to Gus one way or another how he had to pretend to flow the information. The state people didn't think much of Gus's county sheriff people and no doubt would form their own theories and do their own investigation, so Gus wasn't worried about working too hard to impress them. If pretending Gus wouldn't do his job made the governor sleep better at night, then a little white lie never hurt anyone. You can agree to anything with anybody, even the governor.

"You can tell the governor we are all one big happy family!"

"Just remember, Gus, you're the family dog. All these other boys in here are career family members but the voters can return you to the pound at anytime. The way I hear it, you don't have long to go." Having thrown his weight around, Brian collected his boys up and left.

Gus made his formal goodbyes to the weary campus police, who were grimly about to go into an all-night session with a rather angry university president. The president, despite his fancy electronic security, didn't do anything actually positive to prevent these girls from getting themselves into the sticky spot they were in, but he sure had advice for the people that had figured out where the missing girls were. He was your typical blowhard authority figure that blamed the messenger not the perpetrator. Gus had met dozens of them on the job and learned to ignore their stale, unimportant advice. To hell with them all was always Gus's philosophy on the type of "help" to the investigation all of these people bring.

It was now early in the morning, and Gus was sitting alone in the campus police station. He was forced to type out on the computer a formal statement of the likely scenario and place in evidence information he had learned today. He logged it officially, and now everyone in the loop had as much information as him had about the crime. He thought the first thing they would do was waste time their own time talking to these same people all over again, because none of them respected the skills of a local sheriff. It would give Gus a head start on the next phase of the investigation… whatever that was going to be. There was still some feint hope Gus would solve the case by himself and perhaps ride the investigation to reelection. There was also the much more real possibility that it was never going to be solved. A lot of crimes never were.

Gus looked at the little clock on the corner of the computer—4:30 a.m. Gus had an idea to fish for a little more information before giving up on the city. Gus picked up the phone and dialed. The phone rang a long time, but Gus stayed on the line, knowing it would eventually be picked up.

A sleepy voice answered the phone. "This is Marty. Who the hell is calling me at this hour?"

"Marty, my good old pal!" replied Gus, faking friendliness in his voice.

"You better have a real scoop to be thinking of your good friend Marty at this hour. And if you do, Gus, I promise to kiss you. What is it and how many papers do you think it will sell?"

Gus paused a minute to calculate in his mind exactly how much he felt he needed to give Marty to eventually get something of value back. The main gist of the story would be old news soon, so there wasn't too much risk giving out the basics. "They know who the dead girls is: Cherry Colston. It will probably hit the morning newscast, and I think it's going to be a big stink. Her parents are of some means and have already put up a big stink."

"That's it? I've already read that on the wire, and it's already too late to run a new front page now. Do you at least have a bio that I can put up on the paper's Internet site?"

"I was about to send you an unofficial anonymous email with the campus bio of her and a lot of the basic information the police know. Will that do for you scoop-wise?"

"Is that all that there is, or is there stuff you know that the police don't know?"

"I'm not holding back anything. Well, nothing that helpful to the official investigation. I met a nice, hard-working college girl from our neck of the woods. Her name is in the report, but I'd be mighty upset if she was badgered by the press. After all, she is one of our own local girls, Marty."

"Yeah, yeah, I'm the sole source of discretion in the newspaper business when it comes to being kind to nice girls. I need stories about bad girls, so are there any of those? Bad girls, bad boys, sex maniacs? I got papers to sell!"

Gus wondered if he should feed Zak's name to Marty, but he decided to give him a pass since Zak was kind enough to watch Gus drink his Bloody Mary without a single word of complaint. He'd get enough buzz from the city newspapers and state police.

"Well, there was a nutty college kid completely off his head with admiration for Josh Hansen and his 'total information awareness.' He's certainly worth a mention, because while he didn't look like a sex maniac, he had a manic personality. Very easily excited, if you know what I mean. I had to slap him around a bit to calm the situation. He knew about the missing girls too. You ever heard of any of that Internet stuff, Marty? It seemed rather popular on campus, sort of like Chairman Mao was to a certain type back in the old radical days."

Marty sighed over the phone. "Not that worthless Internet smear-site crap. Those hackers steal—or shall I say 'acquire'—information and blanket post it without any thought or reason. They give us newsmen a bad name, if you ask me. They call themselves information libertarians and other new-age journalist lingo. What they are is no-talent hacks that make a good deal of money selling stolen information. They aren't real journalists or revolutionaries; they're just self-promoting 'anarchists' out for a buck."

Gus was starting to fall asleep on the phone and was feeling sort of sorry for having brought up the subject. "Sounds interesting," he lied.

"Interesting? It is bloody well dangerous. People have died and lives have been ruined over the crap they post. A person snaps a picture and sticks it on the Internet, and these sites propel the overreaction to it. Before the person knows it, the photo has gone viral and every idiot that thinks they know the true intentions of the person in the picture will smear the poor sucker. In ten days you can go from no one to the most hated person in the country based on public overreaction to a scenario no one bothers to actually think about.

"Worse, though, is they get real stories and totally waste them. The average person can't see the forest through the trees. If you just dump a whole heap of information on the public, more times than not the real story will get lost in all the details. More to the point, there are people out there in any real story that don't want certain things known. This kind of journalism allows them to make big deals out of extraneous bits of the worthless parts of the data, while the real important parts get lost in the noise. Real journalists don't dump data like that, because they understand there are a lot of powerful others out there looking to control their story. These Internet people let other people write the story for them and get all the credit for doing nothing more than hacking and hosting websites."

"I guess the whole Internet thing is sort of important these days. I bet a person could get awful famous from what you're talking about."

"Gus, the whole world is online these days. When are you going to wake up to the reality of the modern era? You can watch all your baseball games instantly at the click of a button. The game and box score are automatically updated in real time. It's total information awareness, Gus."

"Awe, Marty, you know I love reading the morning box scores in your paper."

"Well, Gus, it warms my heart to hear that, but what am I going to do when all you old morning box-score readers die? I need stories, juicy stories to sway readers to stick around. Are you going to help me craft a story tonight or not?"

"Well, Marty, I guarantee you that I lay awake at night worrying about your story problems. For instance, here's a problem: there wouldn't by chance be any famous Internet people living up here in the big city, would there? You know famous from the YouTube, or Internet porn."

"You think it has something to do with the murder?" asked a suddenly wide awake Marty.

"It might, Marty, it just might," said Gus.

"I'll see what I can dig up for you on that."

Having given away all he cared to, Gus now asked one final practical and important question. "Marty, have you dug up anything more on a certain Lance Daniels and where he might be getting campaign money?"

"Nope. That story is dry, very dry."

"Are you sure?"

"Gus, like I told you, I have got to control my information until I can craft my story. That's called real journalism." And with that Marty hung up.

CHAPTER 3

Gus was done with the city for now, and in the late morning he drove back south to his county. He was too tired to go to bed, so he decided on getting a comfort meal at Constantine's café. The café wasn't actually a good place to eat. But it was the only real option left in town from the old days. Much of the old downtown in the county was now vacant, but two businesses remained rather strong. One was Mike's gas station, and the other was Constantine's café. The two businesses had the convenient luck to be on the side of town closest to the highway and thus got a lot of highway traffic. People on the highway don't need very much: motels, gas, and a quick place to eat. Those were the three best businesses a highway-based economy had to offer, and the exit closest to old downtown offered two of the three.

As far back as anyone could remember, no one in the county knew a Mike that had ever owned the old gas station. The gas station changed hands from time to time, so gas-brand loyalty was generally fleeting at the best. The price was always a little higher than expected, but that was because it was a captive audience that arrived at the station. Around these parts your highway traveler fearful of moving too far off the highway had to take what they could get. The locals were gouged too, which was considered par for the gas station businesses. However, this generally led to the owner of the gas station being one of the least liked people in town. Gus suspected this was why the station was named after someone that never existed.

Gus pulled in to the station to fill up the sheriff truck. The pump blinked a message to pay with his card, but Gus only paid with cash. A normal person would have to prepay to use cash at the pump, but every attendant at the station knew the sheriff by sight. They would turn the pump on for him and let him pay after.

He went inside to pay. He looked over at the newspaper rack and decided to buy a local paper as well. Sure, he had the paper delivered to him at home, but Gus wanted to see it now. Although Marty swore he wouldn't get the story out this morning, Gus knew the story would likely be there. A possible sex maniac was going to sell. Heck, it was just a matter of time before the TV news people arrived, if they weren't here already. Lastly Gus made sure to get the receipt so he could bill the fuel expense to the county.

He popped back outside the station and noticed an unwelcome visitor hanging by his truck. A large man in an expensive, tailored Italian suit and covered with gang tattoos wherever his skin was exposed. The man was well known to Gus as Antonio Victor Minnelli. Why he pretended to be Italian was a mystery not worth the time to find out. He was the chief messenger boy for a Mexican gang.

Gus faked a smile and moved toward his truck. "What a pleasure to see you on my side of the border again."

Hands in his pockets, Antonio circled his head as if he didn't like being on the roadside out in the open. Mike's station was a terrible place to try to be inconspicuous. Not that anyone could fail to notice a three-hundred-pound tattooed Mexican in an expensive Italian suit wherever he decided to hang around in this county.

"You know I wouldn't come here and bother you if Big Gustavo hadn't felt the need after hearing about the terrible news earlier this morning. He sent me up here to make absolutely sure you knew where we stood on this."

Gus held up the paper's front page so Antonio could see. "I took it for granted that the big man was against the murder of pretty, rich women, as I've heard they make some of his best clients."

Antonio faked a laugh back. "But let me make it clear we traffic in guns and not drugs. The rich girls do like the drugs, and our gun trading has nothing to do with this murder. I am here to set that record straight. *Soy un hombre de negocios honesto.*"

"And you didn't come to me when the body was first discovered because...?"

"*No sé.* She had no name. She could have been just anyone. But now Big Gustavo heard that even the governor has spoken on this matter, and this death may cause a lot of misunderstanding. This would not be the first time honest Mexicans suffered because the Mexican drug violence was made an easy scapegoat. We have certain business interests to protect, and I am here to see that they get protection."

Gus folded the paper back under his arm and leaned against his truck while watching Antonio nervously pace around. "So the crime was drug related, huh? That is news to me, as I guarantee you it doesn't say a word about drugs in this here paper or any paper. Do you have news perhaps to tell me?"

Antonio continued pacing around the parking lot and was not quick to answer the question. The hot sun and the pacing made him perspire through his expensive clothing. He stopped dead in his tracks while the silence between the two built. He then slowly pulled out a cigarette. He lit the cigarette with an expensive gold lighter and put it in his mouth. He then put the lighter back into his pocket. He pulled out a piece of paper from his pocket. He read it over. He crumpled the paper up and shoved it into a different pocket. Gus continued to sit there leaning on his truck and wondering when the show would end. The answer seemed obvious, so it was just a matter of time until Antonio let it out.

Antonio took one last long drag on the cigarette and dropped it to the ground. "I don't know why I should tell you this, but I do as I'm told. Yes, Big Gustavo has gotten word that possibly there was a drug complication in this death. He had heard possibly this girl was seen at the Tannehill ranch not long before her death. When we heard this news, she was still nobody to Big Gustavo, you understand, so it was thought this information was not important."

"Was she with anyone else?" asked Gus, trying to sound casually not interested.

Antonio replied, "I am sure I can't say."

"You can't say, but the note you just read could say if you let it, I bet. So how about it, does it have anything further to tell me or not?"

Antonio shook his head no. It wasn't a very convincing head shake. Gus took his cue and opened the truck door. He started up the truck and looked out the window to see what Antonio was doing. Antonio was making a fast waddling retreat around the corner and toward the back of the station. Gus was too tired and hungry to sort out just yet if he had been given real information or dirt to dirty up the local dirt. It was likely dirt, but Gus would have liked to have seen that note just the same. Gus pulled the truck out of the station and headed across the street. A silver sedan car drove into the station as he left.

Across the street from the station sat Constantine's café. The café that was not owned by someone named Constantine. But unlike Mike's there was no intended deception involved in this name. Doreen, the current owner, had been sweet on Gus since way back when they were in grade school together. Gus had eventually been sweet on the woman that became his wife instead. Doreen had settled for Constantine, whose family had owned the café for as long as anyone could remember. Constantine died youngish, of a heart attack or stroke, Gus didn't really care enough to remember which it was. Upon the death Doreen had inherited the café.

Gus took one last look in his rearview mirror to make sure Antonio was gone for good. There was just a silver sedan sitting across the street at the station now and no sign of the local gangs. Satisfied he was finally alone enough to enjoy a meal, Gus stepped out of the truck and went into the café. Gus walked by the "Please wait to be seated" sign and headed toward the booth by the window.

"Excuse me, sir, but the sign clearly says to wait," said a woman in an apron.

"Aw come on, Doreen, you know I can't read."

Doreen grabbed a menu out of the bin then placed it back in. She quickly fixed her hair in the glass of the frozen dessert container and went over to Gus's table. "How's the wife?"

"Still dead," replied Gus.

"Good old consistency. You know, Gus, I believe men are so dull at times. You've been sitting at the same corner table since before I owned this place. You've been ordering the same boring meal even though this café prides itself on its fabulously diverse menu. I can tell you a secret: we woman want a little excitement in our life. Take me, for instance. I want constant variety. Have you ever considered something new?"

"Like what?"

"Well…I used to ask my husband if he liked my new hairstyle. I always like getting a new hairdo. But you know what he would always say when I asked him about it? 'What was wrong with the old hairdo?' Can you imagine that? A lazy and boring lack of imagination is what you men all have. You can't think up any new kind of variety in your life, so you end up doing the same thing over and over every day until you die."

"It was my wife that died, if you remember."

"Yes, I remember. I was saying about variety and how men don't like it…except in relationships maybe. Then you men want to bonk something new each night. In relationships women are true to the same boring man forever and ever, and what use is it if they're dead like mine? I'd say there's a lesson in this somewhere for you, Gus, but I'll let you figure out what it is," finished Doreen with a wink.

"Well, I tell you what, why don't you give me the same boring meal I always get, and I promise to fantasize about a young hot blonde sitting next to me to eat it with," replied Gus.

"I'm hoping this blonde looks a lot like me!" Doreen used that as her exit line and headed off to place the order with her kitchen staff.

Gus made a promise to himself that if his fantasy girl ever looked like Doreen, he'd give up on fantasy women. Luckily his fantasies to date had remained boring and consistent.

Gus took a quick look around the place. There were three other guests busy eating at the counter. Overall it was still a nice-looking place, even if the decor was from the late 1950s. Instead of feeling old and out of date it had a kind of a retro chic feel to it. It was a relic to a time when cars and diners were king. Gus determined there was absolutely nothing interesting happening in the café, and thus he had time to read over the local paper.

The front page had pictures of each of the three missing girls, with Cherry's head X'd out. Classy touch there, Marty, thought Gus. There were some nice quotes from the campus police report. They were some quotes from the state police saying rather terrible things about the county sheriff office's work to date on the case. Last night Gus had worked fast to get his side of the story out, but the state police apparently were hard workers too. Gus flipped over to read the editorials. They contained even more bad news, because someone named Sigmund Smudge had written a rather nice election-related smear about Gus. Gus folded the paper back up as acid flooded his stomach.

Doreen returned to the table with a hot glass pot of steaming coffee. "That's funny. Typical, mind you, but still very funny."

"Looks like normal coffee to me," replied Gus, looking at the pot of coffee eagerly.

"No, stupid, I mean that silver car that keeps passing here every fifteen minutes or so today. They've been driving by all morning. A bunch of tourists, I bet. They probably drove accidentally off the highway at the wrong exit, or worse, they're sightseeing our private little murder. Not that it takes long to get back to the highway from here. I bet you fifty bucks the driver is probably a man that won't stop and ask for directions to the murder site!"

"Men never have to ask for direction because they know their wife will tell them the correct direction he's supposed to be going. At least my wife never stopped telling me directions. I spent my whole life going the wrong way no matter which way I was going," sighed Gus, who continued looking at the coffee pot in high hopes it would soon tilt in his mug's direction.

"Ha, ha, here's your coffee." Doreen poured the coffee into the mug while still watching out the window. "Yeah, they pulled into Mike's station to finally get directions. They should have pulled into here; we got cheaper maps than the station and way better coffee."

"I'll tell you what, Doreen. Why don't you run across the street and tell them that instead of telling me?"

"Drink your coffee." Doreen went off to wait on the other customers.

Gus for the first time turned and stared out the window. The silver car was still there. It looked like two people were sitting in it. They looked like two men to Gus. Although in this day and age you couldn't always tell men from women at this distance. They were just sitting there in the car. It sure didn't look like they were searching for any map. They didn't look lost. No, they looked like two people that found what they were looking for, and it was here across the street. At least here across the street was where they were staring at. Who were they? It was one of life's little mysteries that tended to be more interesting in the end than the answer to who killed who. They were probably repo men, thought Gus. Someone in the restaurant wasn't paying their bills. In this county it could be just about anyone.

There were not many customers here today. This time of day, the place mostly attracted tired truckers coming off the highway. The normal tired-family-traveler crowd and the graying locals wouldn't show again until dinner. Gus looked over the three men sitting at the counter. Yup, Gus thought, for sure they were after one of the truckers. Probably they were doing stupid financial stuff and one of them got behind on the truck payments. Tough life, to have a repo man come and take your truck away. A trucker's cab is his home, his escapism, and his livelihood. A person might be able to lose one of those, but to take all three in one grab was a tough blow.

There were two fat truckers that looked one or two hauls from a heart attack. He ignored them and looked at the skinny one. He was younger and had on better clothes. Yeah, thought Gus, the young stupid one was probably the guy. The idiot bought some fancy clothes to impress some girl instead of making his truck payment. What a waste too, as the poor sap probably didn't even get to second base. Well, a man has to learn his lessons in life.

Gus sipped his coffee and waited for the truck drivers at the counter to get up one by one until there was just the young truck driver sitting alone at the counter. Gus finished off his meal and picked up his coffee mug. He moved from his booth by the window toward the counter and casually sat next to the young trucker.

Gus mustered up his generally ineffective fatherly tone of voice and casually struck up a conversation. "Son, are you in any kind of financial trouble? Don't worry about pride, because, you see, I'm the law in these parts, and I can help you out at least from this little part of the mess while you're in my county."

The young driver signed deeply and turned to face Gus. "Does it show that badly?"

Gus shook his head no. "Not at all, but, you see, I'm a sheriff, and we're used to reading people and spotting troubled souls. I figured they were out there waiting on someone, and you're the only one left in here. Trust me, though. As bad as your troubles seem, there is some other person in this world in plenty of worse trouble right now. So go ahead and tell old Sheriff Gus about it."

"OK. I ain't never thought to telling anybody about them, and they've been eating at me for months. You see, it all started when I was doing a long haul over the interstate. I was supposed to take downtime like the regulations say, but I needed time to fit one more extra haul in that month. I got bills to pay, if you understand what I mean. So I drove over my time limit and kept awake by doing those energy drinks two at a time. They're great to keep a person going. Boy, was I going too. I was going and going, and then in the middle of the night it happened. Well, I say the middle of the night, because the clock read three in the morning. But what is time to them, you understand? Well, them aliens just plume spotted me out on the road alone in the middle of the night."

"You mean you got jumped by illegal aliens in my county?" asked Gus.

"They could have been illegal ones or legal ones at that. I don't know the laws regarding aliens. I didn't think to ask them to see anything official. I hope it doesn't matter to you helping me. All I know is they weren't from around these parts and that they tried to snatch me."

"Now let me see if I understand what you're trying to tell me. A repossession company with foreign and possibly illegal repossession agents tried to repossess your truck right then and there on the interstate at three in the morning? They truly are a group of heartless bastards these days. I guess we sold the country out to all kinds of foreign companies, huh. These days you don't know who ultimately owns your home, auto, or college loan. Scary to think they're out there stalking you like that, but I won't put up with stranding truckers at three in morning in my county," sympathized Gus.

"I don't know about being repossessed. The one time being possessed was enough for me. That's the whole problem, Sheriff. You see, I think they did get to me that night. Maybe it was because it was too late at night or part of payback on some loan or something. I didn't even know the illegal aliens invested in the loan market. The worst part is, I swear, sometimes I can feel them still moving inside me. I'll look real close in a mirror but I can't see them. Yet I feel them crawling all over my face. I pick at them and scratch at them and sometimes it'll go away, but it won't go away for too long."

Gus was momentarily confused by the conversation. Finally he asked, "Could you just for the official record clarify who it was that snatched you again?"

"The space aliens, Sheriff. Maybe the illegal kind, and then again maybe they are these legal financial investment kinds you were talking about. I couldn't tell, as I'm not really versed in aliens. You'd think I'd be an expert, but I never went to college or watched a lot of the History Channel, so I couldn't identify them for you. Maybe if I concentrate, though, I could make a police artist sketch for you."

Gus had suddenly become less interested in the conversation. He had struck up a conversation with a total nutter. "No, that won't be necessary. So these space aliens just snatched you and are now living inside you?"

"That's right, and according to you they might be coming back to repossess me, and here I am already stuck being possessed already. I'd be mighty glad to get rid of them. Is there anything I can do, Sheriff?" asked the young truck driver.

"Kid, do the world a favor and stop doing overnight hauls high on methamphetamines for a while. I think the aliens will leave you alone."

"Do you really think so? I never knew meth attracted space aliens. They don't tell you that at the truck stops when they sell it to you."

"I've never known one person that wasn't helped by not doing meth. Other than that, there's nothing more I, as sheriff, can do for you."

Gus shook his head at another wasted life and went back to his favorite table. The young man looked over his shoulders once or twice at Gus, looking worried. Gus tried not to notice and hoped the young man would soon leave. After drinking one more cup of coffee from Doreen, the young man did leave the café. The silver car was still sitting there with the two men sitting in it. Doreen came over to fill Gus's coffee one last time.

"That kid sounded awful messed up. Not, mind you, that I listened to your totally private conversation with him, but you two both have the kind of voice that carries. You don't think there could really be space aliens inside him?"

"Nah, the idiot took some uppers to do his long haul. Moron's got classic signs of meth addiction. Doreen, you aren't in any financial trouble, are you?" asked Gus.

"Not me, Gus. This place has been paid off for years. Heck, it was already paid for when I married into the franchise. Everything now is pure gravy after I pay the taxes. I still get steady trucker traffic through here, so I make a good living, you understand. Good enough for two…not that I have any ideas."

Doreen leaned over and took a long nosy look out of the window. "Those two clearly aren't lost. They've been waiting on something, haven't they? You think they're drug enforcement looking for the meth drivers?"

"No one is dealing in here. Anyone with half a brain knows where to get drugs in these parts. Nah, I'm an expert sleuth, Doreen, and my expert sleuthing tells me you were right the first time. They're obviously stupid tourists, that's all," assured Gus.

Doreen looked at him with a sigh of relief of a mystery solved and slowly headed off again. Gus looked out the window. They were waiting on someone, and there was only one person left they could be waiting on. Sheriff Gus! He could walk over and ask them. They might work for Antonio, but what was the point of him speaking to Gus if he was going to have men watch him?

Then a single word hit Gus: *reporters*. They were a bunch of damn big-city reporters looking to get more dirt on those poor young women. Probably they heard Gus ate here a lot and they were sitting on the place hoping for a scoop. Well, they weren't getting their dirt from Gus. Marty was a local pest, but at least you had to tolerate the local press, because occasionally he was known to dig up something useful or, better still, hide something harmful. These other guys out there were leeches of society, making money off other people's misfortune and other investigators' hard work. They weren't getting a free ride off old Gus. Down here in his county, there were no free lunches.

Gus was done with his meal. He got up and walked by the cashier station without paying like he always did. He had been coming to Doreen's for over thirty years and he hadn't paid yet.

Gus got in the truck and tilted the rearview mirror to get a good look at the silver car. He then slowly backed out of the café and into the street. The silver car sat there, motionless. Gus nonchalantly and methodically headed down the road. After Gus had built a two-block lead, the silver car sprang to life. Bingo, thought Gus. Well, they found the sheriff, but this sheriff wasn't about to give them anything useful. Gus decided to lose them the easy way. The goal for the moment was stay boring. They wouldn't stick around for too long if all Gus gave them was his normal boring office routine. They sat around watching him eat, so now they could sit around all afternoon and watch him fill out office work. Put that in the front headline all you want, thought Gus. Gus turned and headed into the heart of the older part of town.

Most of the historic downtown was vacant thanks to the series of economic recessions. Places that used to be the deli, the bakery, the grocery, the bookstand, the old five and ten, and the hardware store were all gone. One by one they lost out as the economy failed the region and people shopped further and further from the main city center. In their place were discount dollar stores, check-cashing centers, pawn shops, impromptu bars, liquor stores, and abandoned store fronts. There wasn't any good reason to come down this way unless you worked here. The part of downtown next to the government building was slightly less seedy, at least from nine to five, when the place was full of local government workers. There was the fire station, the city council building, a hospital, a post office, and, of course, the law-enforcement complex.

Gus pulled the truck into the law-enforcement complex. It was just a little sheriff's office that hadn't changed much since the remodeling done in the late seventies. Several deputy sheriff cars were in the parking lot. Gus checked his rearview mirror, but the silver car didn't follow him into the lot. Instead it settled in the lot across the street, where the county morgue and crime lab were established inside a more modern building. The two figures remained in their car, watching Gus.

Once inside and out of their direct view, Gus quickly sprang into action and hurried over to the office window's venetian blinds. Peeking through the blinds, Gus could make out the silver car and the two men; they were clearly men now and were clearly at last getting out of their car. They had a camera and started shooting shots across the street at the law-enforcement complex. Gus wondered how much per diem they got to film nothing of interest. Gus wasn't going to ask them or lead them anywhere more interesting. Gus could spend a day filing paper work on the computer and let them get nothing for their trouble. Hopefully, after the first twenty-four hours they'd buzz off and follow the state boys around. Judging by the other cars in the parking lot across the street, there were plenty of state boys bothering people in the coroner's office.

Gus stepped away from the blinds and headed for his office. He stepped over the body of Deputy Drew passed out in the middle of the floor. Gus felt a little envious of the deputy, as Gus was hoping to get some sleep too. Deputy Costner was standing next to the passed-out body with a perplexed look on his face.

"Sheriff, what are we going to do about this awful mess? A group of us have been debating all morning which of us would have to drive him home and dump him off. He can't just lie on the floor all day. I mean, with all these official state people around, what if someone comes in and sees him?"

"Well, at least he is trying to follow my orders. I did tell him he couldn't lay around passed out in front of the building. I tell you what, Deputy, let's not bring him home and let his father see him like that. We don't need some pencil pusher getting mad at us because his son is an idiot. We all know this will be our fault. Just get a couple deputies and prop him up in his office until he wakes up. If you want to, you guys got my permission to spit on him, but I don't think that deputy is worth the spit."

"The rest of us are overworked because we got to carry his dead weight."

"I know, I know, but it is all about politics, son. Long after I'm gone, that sack will still be here because of politics, so you guys do the best you can."

"Can we stick him in the drunk tank?" asked Costner.

"Nah, I don't want him smelling up the higher-class personnel in there."

Costner frowned a little and went off to fetch another deputy to move the passed-out drunkard. Gus continued on his way from the entrance to his office door. Lupita was sitting at her desk and appeared to be happily waiting for him to arrive.

"Former sheriff, have you seen today's editorial page? You're the star! The paper says that you are mucking up the official investigation and placing the whole town at the peril of dangerous unknown assailants. Even better, the afternoon news on TV says a talented and gifted young student at the college is accusing you of assault! It is just like you to strike a future genius for no reason. Don't you know the children are our future? Well, at least the children smart enough to live to adulthood and not get killed by sex maniacs," said Lupita, trying to hand over her copy of the paper with the Smudge editorial highlighted in yellow marker.

The sheriff reluctantly took the paper out of Lupita's hands and quickly glanced over the page, pretending to read it. It was no fun telling Lupita he had bought the paper and seen the editorial already. Anyways, he's the one that told the press about the college thing last night. Seemed like a good idea at the time. A nice distraction to keep them from harping on the fact they really didn't know where the other two girls were. The press liked shiny things, and if you shook some in front of them, they might forget the real story. It was exactly like what Marty had told him last night, and they both knew it worked sometimes.

The editorial was a different matter, though. The name Sigmund Smudge concerned citizen was at the bottom of the editorial. The name didn't mean anything to Gus when he glanced at it this morning, and it still meant nothing. Gus tossed the paper back onto her desk.

"Who the hell is Sigmund Smudge, and what makes him an authority in law-enforcement matters?"

"He doesn't like you, so he is clearly a wise and concerned citizen. The TV reporters were here earlier, and they don't like you either," replied Lupita.

"Few people do, Lupita, few people do. Oh, by the way, the state police and probably the city police are now involved in the case. They don't like me either, and that feeling has been mutual for years. If they happen to call, tell them that I'm out."

One office member was completely incapacitated and another was completely hostile. At least today felt like a normal day. Things might be looking up for old Sheriff Gus.

Gus went through his office door. Lupita used that moment to get the last word in. "If the state police comes, I will tell them you are a lazy criminal son of a bitch and the best thing they can do for this county if they want to clean it up would be to arrest you."

Gus sat down at his desk. The lack of sleep the night before was overcoming him now. He looked at the inbox on the desk. There were a few sheets of paper in there. He wearily picked up the papers out of the box. It was a fax from the campus parking attendants for the night the three girls went missing. They had the plate numbers, the make of car, color, and the registration numbers for the automobiles that got logged the night the women were last seen. Those little ticket writers were pretty thorough, but there wasn't any limited-edition Mercedes on the list, blue or otherwise. Their eagle eyes must have missed the car. Gus looked over the blue cars on the list, but none of them seemed a credible mistake for a reliable eyewitness. Mandy was his only true credible witness at this point, thought Gus. So he felt honor bound to believe her over the ticket trolls that patrolled the campus parking lots. Until further information came his way, the car information was useless to him. Gus tucked the fax into his manila folder. It was more information but it wasn't clear the information was adding up to any hot leads.

Gus went over to the water jug and filled a paper cup. He tried pacing a little in the office to stay awake. He wanted to do something, but what was left for him to do? There were two eager beavers outside waiting for him to lead them to a story, but at the moment there was nowhere to go. Gus's plan was to not give them anything anyways, so in that regard everything was working out.

Gus sat back down and thought over the case as he saw it. Somewhere in his county there were two missing attractive daughters of rich families. Then again, they need not be still here, and Gus had not a clue where to look to find out one way or another. He had two cars that might have been together and the make and color of one of them and the color of the other. He had a very vague description of the suspect. He had a fat fake Italian drug stoolie telling him stories that might mean something. And he had about another month or so to figure it all out before Lance had his chance to fail to solve the case.

Suddenly Gus was standing in a broad, open pasture. In the distance ran a barbed wire fence. Gus could make out an opening in the fence and slowly drifted effortlessly through the air toward it. As he drew closer, he could make out that the opening in the fence was a window. There were two figures sitting in front of the window. One was a striking blonde. She sat with another person, whose appearance at first wasn't clear. Gus noticed the figure had a steaming cup of hot coffee. Gus started to drift like a falling feather toward the seated couple. As Gus came within range of the striking blonde, she turned—Doreen in a cheap prom dress and heavy makeup. Disappointment filled Gus, and he sank into the mud below his feet.

Gus focused his eyes on the other figure seated with her. He was a nebulous white blob reading a paper. He introduced himself to Gus as Mr. Sigmund Smudge. The figure then howled a jackal-like laugh until he coughed from exhaustion. Up from his innards came money, lots and lots of money, until it filled the pasture. Gus was so distracted by the sight of all that money that he failed at first to notice that the two figures had turned to stare out the window. Gus looked out the window, but to his mounting frustration he could see nothing. The window was covered in a layer of mud. Gus wiped at the mud with the paper the blob was reading. The mud turned red, blood red. In desperation Gus throw the coffee onto the window, and the blood-red mud dissolved. The window was now transparent. On the other side, far in the distance, was a blue car. In the car was a sign propped up in the window. Gus could feel he was running now through the window and toward the car. The harder he ran, the faster the car seemed to move from him. Gus chugged harder and the car came ever slightly closer and closer until the sign came into full view. Larger and larger the words grew in the frame of Gus's sight until the sign and the words filled Gus's total field of view. The sign read Vote for Sherriff Gus.

Terrance barged into the office and startled the sleeping Gus. It was such a start that Gus accidentally crushed the water-filled cup next to his hand and water spilled all over Gus and his desk.

"Jesus, Gus, did you really strike an unarmed college kid?"

"Thanks, Terrance. After a good day's sleep I needed a bath anyways. You know, this is my sheriff's office, and you could knock or have Lupita page me before just popping in here. And what's this entire ruckus about striking a kid? Does that sound like your good friendly Sheriff Gus to you? Of course I never struck any kid."

"Aw shit, Gus, that's too bad. The polling shows our demographic is trending toward the older and more bitter voters. They generally despise young college age kids. Over ninety percent of our base approves of physical punishment for children in school. This college beating story is getting huge raves within our base."

Gus was dabbing the water on his desk with paper towel. "I didn't know I had a base. Now that I do know them, I must admit they sound like the kind of people I was happier about when they were strangers. Anyways, to clarify, it wasn't a beating I didn't do, it was at most two punches that I didn't do. I just want to make that clear if it matters to the base."

"Aw, Gus, it don't matter. Just as long as you don't go announcing the story was a lie. Deny it in mixed company, sure, but when talking to the base don't forget to mention we are pro being tough on youth violence. Better yet, just mention the words *youth violence*, as polling suggests our voting base is motivated out of fear of the young in general."

Gus got up from the wet desk to find some more paper towels. He dabbed one towel after another, now trying to dry himself off. "Why can't anyone make a paper towel that absorbs worth a damn? So you ran over here in a huff and woke me from my first real sleep in over thirty-six hours to tell me to beat more county children in order to win this election? Was that a message really worth this watery mess?"

"What! No, no. I came over here to find out if it was true that we now have state and federal people coming to take this investigation away. Do you understand what this means? All you have to do is solve this case before the rest of them, and we got the national media on our side. That's huge for putting our newfound opponents in their place! The boys sent me over here to tell you they want you to solve this case for the good of the county."

A wave of exhaustion came over Gus, and he gave up on the paper towel idea. He tossed it in the direction of the waste basket—it missed— and, still damp, he wandered over to his desk and sat down. The whole idea of solving the case to save the election, of course, had occurred to him.

"Great, Terrance, now all I have to do is solve a murder and a double kidnapping with all the clues I've secretly stashed away until you came here and told me to use them."

"Really?"

"No, not really! Naturally I've understood I need to kill this dead girl story personally or this office is going to be done in. I've been working as best I can on it and have been trying to stay ahead of the state people. But let us face an important fact: I ain't never solved a real murder in my life, and we both know that. What makes you think I'm going to solve this mess before the election? The media is making hay out of one dead pretty girl, just wait until it is three dead pretty girls!"

"Gus, you got to do this for us. We got to maintain control of this county, or imagine what could happen. There could be two political parties for people to choose from!"

Gus imagined that actually there would just be different names skating by on parking and speeding tickets and someone's idiot son would have to sleep it off inside the drunk tank rather than outside it. The new boss wouldn't be different than the old boss.

Gus opened the top drawer of his desk. He grabbed a handful of fliers out of it. They all in one way or another had Lance's name on them and said rather horrible things about Gus.

"Terrance, while we are talking about me helping you to win this election for the boys, what the hell are the boys doing about this? Where the hell is he getting the money to mail five or six fliers a day to my house? I've been gone up to the city, so I can only imagine how many more of these are waiting at home for me. Do you understand I can't listen to my answering machine because Lance Daniels is now the only human being that calls?"

Terrance looked it over. "I know, Gus, but don't worry. The boys are coming up with a mailer or two of our own. I can't tell you where his money is coming from, but trust me, the boys are planning a very powerful counterpunch, just as soon as we figure out how to pay for it."

Gus rubbed his temple in pain. They were losing the race badly. He felt like punching Terrance, but Terrance was unfortunately the wrong age to help Gus's standing with his base. The phone rang and allowed Gus to ignore Terrance.

"Hello, this is the sheriff's office, can you please hold for a brief minute?" Gus turned to Terrance. "Terrance, I have official business here, so if you would please excuse me, this is a very important phone call." He didn't really want to talk to anyone on the phone, but at least it would free him from Terrance and the doomed political race.

"Sure, Gus. And make sure to get a paper tomorrow. We got a staunch editorial about our pro-spanking-in-school stance ready to run. From county line to county line, every elderly man with a walker will know Sheriff Gus will keep the kids off his lawn. You'll see the boys are on top of everything."

Terrance rushed out of the office and Gus turned his attention back to the phone.

"It's Sheriff Gus here at the sheriff's office, sorry for that slight delay."

"This is Dr. Armstrong, the coroner here at the coroner's office. I got good news for the sheriff at the sheriff's office."

Gus couldn't tell for sure, but it felt like Chloe was making a little joke about him. "News already! You usually don't say anything on the record until all the tests are in. It's not like you to give me information off the record."

"Well, then this would be unofficial news. You have the state police to thank, because they were here today bothering me."

"They gave you the usual warm state welcome."

"They're a bunch of arrogant assholes. Not just one or two, I mean the whole lot of them. You'd think I'd gotten my degree from a Cracker Jack box the way they talked down to me. They think of us county people as just short of the cast of *Deliverance*. They took their own samples and reviewed all the evidence and logged it again. Then they took their own photographs of the murder scene. They said I am no longer needed. Me! I'm the coroner, and I'm not needed on the most important case in this county since anyone can remember! Well, they can't take our jurisdiction away, and they aren't going to intimidate me from doing a good job on this case."

"So you called your good friend sheriff Gus to complain about them? Trust me, Sheriff Gus is totally with you on this. I'm sure you are aware that I have countless years of experience being told I'm a hayseed by some of the dumbest "state" people the Earth has to offer."

"I actually really have something important to tell you. Had they been nicer, they'd have something too, but now they can stick it until the official report come out."

"You can't exactly hide evidence from the state police," explained Gus.

"I'm not hiding anything. It's in the documents and samples I gave them. They'll just have to figure it out for themselves, because they are ignoring all our documentation and doing it all again themselves. That's what they wanted, so that's what they're getting. Trust me, I offered it all to them."

Gus was always impressed with Dr. Armstrong's ability to get to the heart of the friendly problem of cooperation within the happy family that was law enforcement. "I see, and in the meantime what news is there?"

"I found a little glass jar in an evidence bag marked 'victim's back pocket.' I never bagged that item, and I don't know who did. More interesting is, I'm pretty sure the little vial has meth in it. And there were no fingerprints on it."

"Holding or was she taking it?"

"Gus, you know I'll have to wait for the blood results to answer that. But it's hard to put a vial of meth in your pocket without touching it and leaving prints of some kind. Particularly if you have no back pockets. Remember, the girl was in yoga shorts."

"I'll admit that it has been a while sine my last yoga class. So you think it was planted. Did you give this vial to our friends in the state police so they can't say we are withholding evidence?"

"Of course I did, why do you keep asking me that?"

"Had to know for sure who touched what and had what when. That murder site was very clean. Someone planted a vial of drugs on her after the fact. Is it the same person that cleaned the rest up real pretty to give us no other clues? Sure wish I knew who was around these parts that could or would do that and why they went to the bother."

"But if the vial really has meth in it, then that might give you a hint, right?" asked Dr. Armstrong.

"Yeah, I got the hint. Thanks for letting me in on this thing; it might help me out a lot."

"I didn't do it for you. I did it for the victim. The state police seem only to care about the TV cameras in the capitol."

"OK, Chloe—I mean Dr. Armstrong. Just don't let them get to you. They care, I think, but they got to put up an act. We all got to put up a good act. Either way they'll be gone in a few days, so long as nothing exciting happens."

Gus quickly hung up the phone. Suddenly he had a convergence of evidence all telling him the same thing. He had Antonio telling him the murder was drug related. His neat and tidy helper had left evidence intentionally to say it was drug related. Was the vial overlooked on the victim on the day she was found, or was it planted possibly as late as today? It's not like Antonio couldn't bribe someone in the state police to plant the stuff.

There were also a lot of easily bribed reporters hanging around; he left at least two of them outside the morgue.

Well, they wanted him—heck, were begging him—to talk to the drug gangs. He didn't know why they wanted him to do it, but there was really only way to find out. He was going to talk it over with the drug people—but their rivals wanted the conversation to happen too badly. So Gus was going to punish them and have them wait. Gus would follow their lead but not today. Today they were going to have to cool their heels outside getting nothing interesting.

Gus walked over to the filing cabinet again. He took out the county phone book. He plunked it back down on his desk. He started leafing through it. He got to the S section. No Smudges, Sigmund or otherwise, were to be found. That was the problem with this town: just when one mystery started to move, another popped up without a solution. Who was Sigmund Smudge, and why did he hate Sheriff Gus?

Gus couldn't advance any further on the subject, because Terrance burst back into the office with Deputy Costner, carrying a large sign. It was a cardboard cutout of a rather handsome man in a sheriff uniform. The cutout was holding a sign that said Vote GUS for Sheriff.

"Who the hell is that?" asked Gus in disgust.

"It's you. Isn't it great? We are going to put these in storefronts all over town."

"It doesn't look like you," pointed out the deputy.

"That's some good detective work, Deputy. Terrance, I thought we were going with a younger photo of me, not a young photograph of some-one that is not me."

"Look, Gus, it doesn't really matter who is on the sign. I mean, who really knows what their local sheriff looks like but felons that can't vote anyways?"

"I've got a dead girl, two missing ones, a newspaper posting smear editorials, and an opponent with charisma, billboards, daily fliers, robotic phone callers, and an apparently endless mountain of cash. Now I don't even have me in the campaign anymore! I was the one thing I was counting on in this whole mess."

"Don't worry, Gus. I've never lost a campaign for you yet."

While this was technically true, the assurance did nothing to end Gus's worry about his future employment. Gus walked over to the cardboard cutout that wasn't him and put his cowboy hat on it.

"I'm leaving Gus Junior in charge here. I've got some official sleeping to do. If anyone comes with any new law-enforcement problems, you just tell them young fake Gus Junior would love to hear all about them."

With that, Gus left the office to chase down some much-needed sleep.

CHAPTER 4

The Tannehill Ranch was out in the heart of prime county ranch land. The ranch part of the Tannehill Ranch was in name only these days. While Old Man Tannehill had left the land in pretty good condition for Rex, his oldest son, Rex didn't take well to the ranching business. Rex was known to run the herd side of the ranching business just fine, but not the money aspect of the business. It wasn't long before Rex got in with the anti-tax cults that prayed on gullible small-business owners. They had, for just a small monthly fee, explained to Rex the evils of the federal government and a complex system that allowed a job creator to avoid paying lifeblood-robbing taxes to such a government. Rex started on the race to the bottom, paying his hired help less and less until he paid the lowest wages around. Meanwhile he banked all the profit in the special anti-tax bank accounts the cults told him to use. That and he remembered to pay his monthly fees to keep up his special tax status. Eventually word got around town that the internal revenue service was on the lookout for Rex. The too-good-to-be-true scheme to avoid taxes turned out—to no one's surprise but Rex's—to be a pyramid scheme that made money for those on top and left Rex facing criminal charges on tax evasion.

Lucky for the Tannehill family, Rex died before they lost the ranch. While hiding in Juarez from the IRS, Rex had gotten in an argument at a bar with a local gang member. The gang member had boasted that he could name all five members of the Spice Girls. Rex doubted he could. It was not known for sure why he doubted this, although he was rumored to have been both drunk and stupid at the time of this ten-dollar wager. When the gang member claimed he had won the bet, Rex, being Rex, refused to pay up. Thus, in the end, Rex lost both his ten dollars and his life to a drunken barroom knife fight. The bitter irony in the story as the Tannehill family tells it was that the gang member had misidentified Emma Bunton as Emma Button, so Rex was right on technicalities. But that didn't matter so much after the fifteenth knife wound.

Stupid was supposed to run in the Tannehill family children, so little was expected of the next son in line to inherit the Tannehill Ranch, Trash Tannehill. Trash had no interest or intention of running a ranching business. Lucky for him by the time he inherited it from his late brother there wasn't much of a business left to inherit. Trash had his brother Rex's greed for money, but he also had the brains to find a business the family could make money at. The new ranch business was more in line with Trash's personal expertise.

Prior to his inheritance, Trash had moved out of the county and into the city. He had no love for his father or his useless government-avoiding brother. In fact, instead of avoiding the government, not long after going to the city Trash was serving time at the government's expense in one of its many for-profit prison facilities. Prison life, however, was good for a criminal to meet other criminals and discus and improve on the criminal trade. Prison for Trash was sort of a college for the illicit arts, and he earned his diploma. It was much like any other college, only with cleaner dormitories and a higher rate of rape. Once out of prison, Trash used his newfound skills and his newly inherited land to set up a medical marijuana farm on the ranch. It was good business, and the poor rural area was prime territory for a solid drug den, even if it had stiff foreign competition from the south.

Foreign competition had its advantages to a local pot farmer. County powers had known about the drug farm for several years now, but they did nothing to end it. They figured they could close it down anytime they needed to, but they had to admit there were advantages to leaving it open.

Trash's fierce defense of his business kept the Mexican drug cartels out of the county. While the good citizens of the county sure hated their drug dealers when they weren't secretly buying from them, they hated and feared the Mexicans more. Well, when they weren't hiring them to landscape for them, do construction for them, nanny for them, run the ranches for them, and do maid service and just about every other dirty job in the county. In the good old days, the hatred was strictly along racial lines. Today the county was actually half Mexican by heritage, and most of them were born and raised legal Americans. But that didn't really change things. The Mexican cartels gave the Mexican-Americans a bad name and made life bitterly hard for them, so, as it turned out, they hated the cartels more than anyone in the county. So while everyone knew the drugs were there on Trash's ranch, no one seemed to really care enough about it to make sure they weren't there.

So, if someone was trying really hard to tell Gus that local drug traffic was involved in the murder, then there was really only one place to go. He turned off the police band because he didn't want something unimportant distracting him from his current task. He had deputies to deal with the penny-ante stuff. If something really important happened, they'd call.

Gus drove by the Tannehill Ranch land, watching a river of cannabis plants flow by his truck's windows. Gus knew that the medical pot stuff was just a cover for the real operations of the ranch. Sure, pot made money, but today's modern drug business was all about methamphetamines. Somewhere on the ranch there was a lot of it being made out of sight of the average local passerby. The ranch was heavily guarded by heavily armed local boys. Gus knew Trash would have at least two boys stationed around the driveway, and those boys would be carrying, at minimum, shotguns.

Gus slowed the truck to a crawl as he approached the driveway so the boys could get a good look. They parted at the sight of the local sheriff. Everyone on the ranch knew Gus and his truck by sight. Gus chuckled to himself as he passed them. The head drug dealer does one thing besides making drugs and fighting other drug dealers to keep the territory to make drugs: he keeps order in his own gang, and that meant each boy at the gate was likely voting the right way. The whole ranch would be voting for Gus so long as Gus kept Trash happy. The powers that be tolerated Trash and his crew and forced Gus to tolerate them too. Gus personally didn't give a damn about any one of them. He would put them all in jail if only anyone would bother to prosecute them. But no one would, so there wasn't much point of an arrest.

Gus stopped the truck at the entrance to the driveway of the ranch. The boys on either side of the truck were checking him out to make sure the sheriff was actually in the truck marked "Sheriff." They were carrying assault rifles and weren't afraid to point them straight at Gus. Gus rolled down the driver's window just to make sure the boys got a real good look at who he was.

"I hope those guns were all made in America, boys! When they find your corpses in a shallow grave out there in the desert I don't want them federal law-enforcement officers thinking that my county boys carried any of those foreign-made weapons. Americans make the best guns in the world, and, because of that, some of the finest corpses."

"Aw, sheriff, I don't know. Do they stamp a label on these things?" replied one of the confused gunners, turning his gun over looking for a Made in the USA stamp. Another guard signaled Gus past the welcome party with a wave of his middle finger. What a nice group of boys—nice and stupid, thought Gus. They were taking all the risk, and Trash Tannehill made most of the profits. A drug gang is a great way to make a little money before stopping off at the grave. It isn't much different than most low-paying jobs with no benefits: you do all the hard work, and someone else makes all the profits. Your death generally comes at a vastly accelerated rate, so the lack of healthcare never really matters.

Gus recognized the dull guard as Samantha Owens's second youngest. Good ol' Johnny Owens sure was making his momma proud. The last time Gus saw him he was about ten. Gus remembered him as a cute kid. Well, we're all cute at that age, he thought. Now he was a drug dealer, and a low-rate one at that. Next time Gus saw his momma at least he could tell her that little Johnny was working.

At the top of the driveway were a few more armed men hanging around. They were less heavily armed than those below but no less

84

curious to see the local sheriff. Gus could see the main ranch complex from his truck window. The complex was composed of two large barns and the old-style family house. The house was built by Great-Grandpa Tannehill with his own hands. He'd probably be rolling over in his grave if he knew what the ranch had become. Gus figured this was particularly true because Trash hadn't bothered to keep his great-granddaddy's gin still in working operation. Each generation had its own personal recreational poison product, but why on Earth people continued to do these new destructive drugs when good old whiskey worked just as well was beyond Gus's power to understand. All he knew was they did it, and there was a lot of money to be made because of it. The place didn't look like money from the outside, but Gus knew Trash had heaps of it stored away out of sight.

Gus saw Trash Tannehill sitting on his porch drinking a cheap domestic lite beer. He was a skinny guy in a plain button-down cowboy shirt and a pair of jeans. The guy could afford anything he wanted but wasn't classy enough to want something better tasting. Gus got out of the truck and walked slowly and carefully toward Trash. The two of them were as a general rule on friendly terms. All the same, they weren't very nice to each other. Trash waved Gus up to the porch like they were good-old-boy drinking buddies.

"I see the crop is really growing in this year. No doubt another medical miracle is just about to be harvested."

"Why thank you, Gus. I see your eyes still work. If you ever get glaucoma you know where to come. I want you to know I personally contributed ten whole dollars to your reelection campaign. If there is one candidate in this county that understands the need for medical marijuana patients, I thought it must be you. I've never seen a sicker man in my life to occupy a sheriff's office than my good old friend Sheriff Gus," replied Trash, still holding the lite beer in his hand.

"Well, I thank you for your support. I'm sure all my constituents will be glad to know the county's leading job creator is fully behind my reelection. I heard from a mutual acquaintance that you might have been creating a few more jobs just recently, as a matter of fact."

Tannehill pulled a fresh lite beer from a cooler by his feet. "Well, business is murder, you know, so I can't tell for sure when a new job opportunity will just happen to open up. Right now I can assure you my business is completely booked to capacity, so our mutual acquaintance has been steering you wrong. Do you want a beer, Sheriff, or are you one of those people that can't hold their beer when on duty?"

"I don't think there's much chance of being seen here." replied Gus. Gus was tired of the long-distance exchange and strolled up to the porch. He pulled a beer out of the cooler, sat down in a chair next to Tannehill, and started to drink.

"So you aren't here on any other official basis, just inquiring into potential future job opportunities?"

"Now I get confused which of the barns has the guns in it. I've always been told it was the longer barn. You know, the one with the heavy padlock on it and the armed guard standing in front. I always found it funny that they claim you're in some type of war with the Mexican cartels, yet you are also a prime source of weapons to these same gangs. The gangs then use these guns to kill your own boys…"

"Yeah, life can be pretty funny. But we both know you ain't here to talk about my guns," offered Trash, flexing his rather puny biceps.

"More to the point, then, I heard you might have sold some drugs to a few girls down from the city on a lark. Now I'm just saying I might have heard you did this. You might not have. But as sheriff I do have to ask the tough, pointed questions. I was thinking maybe one of the girls or someone they were with is or was working with you? I've heard this might be true, and there is some evidence this might be true. Not strong evidence, and I would say probably planted evidence, but it is evidence all the same."

"I sell a lot of drugs to a lot of girls. I can't remember every loser that buys a dime bag off one of my boys. I send a load of drugs up north to the city once a week, twice during the holiday season, when people are feeling extra festive. One girl, two girls, three girls…I got a dozen up there selling it and thousands buying it. I couldn't possibly know every face that works and worked for me. I'm sure the direct answer to what you're asking about is a firm 'I don't know.'"

"I believe they bought the stuff down here, locally, or else why would Antonio know about it? They were driving a very nice, blue, limited-edition Mercedes driven by, I imagine, a rather good-looking man. The man is the type you might remember if you saw him. I know our mutual friend Antonio or one of his boys got a good look and remembers the car," explained Gus.

"Well, maybe you should keep asking him about it and not me," replied Trash in a friendly but angry voice.

"I didn't ask Antonio anything; he came to me. I imagine it was to sell you out over this situation you now find yourself in. I imagine he knows these people had contact with you and it might be enough to get the federal boys to bust this here lovely and idyllic wonderland ranch. So did you see the dead girl ever? More important, perhaps you recognized this person she was with?"

"You know, I did think I had seen him before…"

"Where?" asked Gus.

"There was a second car, you know. It was a black car that sat at the end of the driveway and wouldn't come up here to help make the buy. The guy was a pretty handsome dude. He bought a shit load of drugs from me. I mean, enough to last him a year or two. I thought maybe he was going into dealing it—"

"But you wouldn't have sold it to him for that. You don't want a guy like that dealing it, because if he got caught, he wouldn't be scared enough to stay quiet. So you must have known who he was and why he was buying so much of your product," pointed out Gus, as he slowly patted the beer on his tummy.

Tannehill delayed answering. He pulled back on his beer for a while. He finished it and tossed it off the porch. One of the boys ran over and picked it up and carried it off. Finally Tannehill spoke, "That's the difference between you and me. My control doesn't depend on popular opinion. Do you want to tell me my job or listen? So this black car that didn't come up the driveway. The boys got suspicious, so slick like a cat they went down through the bushes to the end of the property and got the license plate number. That number wouldn't interest you, would it?"

"It might. But I imagine you got enough resources to check it out yourself and can already tell me how interesting the plate number is."

Gus had finished his own beer during the long pause while Trash had downed his. Gus reached down to the cooler and got another one. Tannehill unbuttoned his shirt pocket and took out a piece of paper. He unfolded it, held it up to his face, and took a long look at it. He placed the paper on the cooler at both of their feet.

"I checked it out, all right, but it wasn't registered to any drug dealer known to me. It was a company car of all things. Guy must be a complete fake. Never heard of the company it was registered to, but it was up north somewhere. Way too far up north to be connected to any business around here. So what does this company want in this county, or did this guy steal it and use it to pick up the three chicks? I can't find the guy anymore to ask him, and, well, the only chick anyone's seen can't speak much. I figure you might know the answers to my questions, though."

"That building across from the armory is your drug lab, isn't it? You said they bought some hard drugs, and I imagine it wasn't just medical seed for his glaucoma."

"You know what's what and where it all is—Did you see that, Sheriff?"

Tannehill suddenly stood up, very alarmed and agitated. He shaded his eyes and looked out into the large marijuana field that surrounded the ranch. He pointed over to some of his boys. The boys broke off from guarding the house and moved into the field. They had their guns off their shoulders and into their hands, ready for action.

Gus took the opportunity to pick up the piece of paper from the cooler and put it into his own pocket. "Now, Trash, don't you go changing the subject all the time. We were discussing, I believe, the man with the three young women. I believe you could tell me a little more about him. You took that black car's plates down, so it is logical to conclude you took down the other number too."

Trash was still too distracted to properly hear the sheriff. "What, Sheriff? I'm sorry for the commotion, but I do have a business to run. I saw a glint of light flashing in my fields, probably a pair of field glasses. Freaking Gustavo's gang trying to rob me. I deal them guns to keep them happy enough so they won't totally wipe me out of business. Still here it is today I've got information from you confirming they have been spying on me. There is a surprising amount of dishonesty in the drug business. They would kill me as sure as I would kill them if the opportunity arose. Even better for them is sticking me with some total bullshit murder wrap because some guy offs his bitch with my drugs. You're lucky to have me around, Sheriff. Some guys out there are pure animals. Heck, they don't even speak good American like me." Tannehill motioned out in the field for his boys to move in a different direction.

Sheriff Gus finished off his second beer. "I didn't see anything out there a minute ago. Maybe you're just getting paranoid. Guilt over murder will do that to a man, but so will certain drugs. I hope for your sake you aren't using your own product line." Of course Gus already knew he was a user. The signs of abuse were all over his and his boys' faces.

Tannehill looked over his shoulder at Gus. "Everyone in this county says you are a lazy good-for-nothing sheriff. You know, I think they're all wrong. You ain't so dumb as you appear to be. You're as good a sheriff as you want to be."

"Correction: I've always been as good a sheriff as they *let* me be. If I were a really good sheriff, everyone's asses would be in jail, and that includes mine."

Tannehill laughed as the boys came out of the field empty handed.

"Looks like your boys didn't find your snoop," Gus said.

"Not this time. But we've caught our share in the past, don't you worry. I got bodies buried out in the desert where you'll never find them. They'll be back and they'll be caught."

Johnny came running up to the porch. "Sheriff, the radio in your truck is squawking non-stop. I think you better answer it."

Gus didn't want to leave. He felt there was more information to get out of Tannehill. He didn't think that dead girl was a snooper Trash found on his land. She'd never be found if that was true. Still, Gus had a feeling Trash knew more than what was on that paper. Antonio, however, was going to be disappointed there didn't appear to be enough here to bring the law down on this place as of yet. A peaceful drug buy wasn't enough to move Trash back into prison, at least not in this county.

Gus asked, "What about it is so important that I have to rush off this chair?"

"I think someone else is dead, Sheriff! A deputy said something about another girl being found at Ernie's farm. He was hollering to move your bottom, as the state police was already there and you were missing out. He was hopping mad, said they were freezing the county out of it again."

Tannehill started to laugh hard. He grabbed a beer from the cooler and tossed it to Gus. "Looks like you're going to need this. Three girls come down south, and now there is only one little girl left. They're dropping like flies in this county these days. I'd hate to be the incumbent running for office, with a drug-addicted, sex-maniac murderer about. The news will be all over the Internet for sure. A guy running for your job could get an awful huge boost if he did an honest business man like me a favor and found the murderer." Trash laughed again at Gus, got a beer for himself, and sat down.

Gus guzzled the rest of his third beer, threw it onto the ground, and headed back to the truck. He felt there was something important that was left unsaid between the two of them. There was the matter of the blue car and whether Trash had its license plate; then again, maybe it was something else. Drug dealers only gave you as much help as they felt was needed to keep themselves operational. Perhaps Tannehill was planning to make a buck or two off the murderer too.

Well, neither of them planned on going anywhere soon, and there was a dead body waiting for him. There was always time to renew acquaintances with Trash at a later date.

Reluctantly Gus drove the truck once again to Ernie's ranch. This time he knew what to expect. He knew another young woman was dead, he knew where she was from, and he had a fifty-fifty guess as to her name. Gus also knew that the crime scene this time would be a zoo of state, possibly federal, and county workers. Each one stepping on the other's toes trying to take jurisdiction. The local media and the state media would also be there. The thought of another negative round of headlines was more than Gus could stomach. But expectations aren't always met to one's dissatisfaction.

As he approached the likely crime scene, the crowd he expected failed to materialize by the roadside. All he could see was Deputy Drew's squad car sitting on the side of the road. There wasn't another soul around. Perhaps Drew had been mistaken and there was no second murder. Drew was waving his arms madly at the sight of Gus. Something must be up. Gus pulled the truck up and got out.

"Deputy, where is everyone? I thought there was supposed to be a big commotion going on here."

"Sorry, Sheriff, I was a little slow on the draw, and, well, you just plum missed all the excitement. You should have seen it about an hour ago, though. There were state police, forensic people, and that hot female coroner all over this place. I can't wait to see if I made the evening news. All the big television stations from the city were down here covering the story. It was so exciting I forgot to call you right away. But, boy, you should have seen it."

"I *should* have. Why didn't you call me earlier? This was or is my investigation too."

"Well, I meant to call you earlier. I was on desk duty"—which meant he was sprawled out asleep on his desk, Gus thought—"when this call came in saying there was another body found out here at the ranch. I thought, 'Man, poor Ernie is going to have to fix two cut fences in one week.' I was standing right there thinking that I had to call the sheriff and tell him to get here fast, but then I got absorbed into some desk work."

"I hope you don't mean you slept a little more."

"I was doing nothing of the sort! I tried to log it on the computer, and, well, I found our machine has solitaire on it. Time just passed quickly. Anyways, I figured it didn't matter, since she was already dead when the call came in. I figured that she couldn't get more deader while I was doing important computer work. So after a few more games, I decided to come up here and take a look. And then it was so busy I forgot to call you again. But I figured it was all over the police band radio so you must have known. It all turned out as I expected it would, so don't you worry; by the time I got here, she was still dead. She was a pretty disgusting mess, Sheriff, let me tell you."

"I'm listening, so don't feel you have to stop for dramatic pauses," replied Gus.

"When I finally got here, the body was already in the meat wagon to take her away. I was all happy, as I generally hate seeing dead people. They're kind of creepy, and you're never sure they won't become a zombie. So I'm feeling all good about being able to miss out seeing the body when the state police guys end up betting me twenty bucks I would throw up if I looked at her. Well, twenty bucks is good drinking money, so I had to take the bet. I mean, for the sake of the reputation of our department I had to take the bet. So I went into the coroner car and pulled back the sheet to have a peek at her.

"She was an awful mess, Sheriff. When I say 'mess' what I mean is she was all torn up like. She had some teeth missing, torn out whole from the jaw. Someone had smashed her little fingers and toes with a hammer. I mean each one was smashed. They were just meaty little blobs dangling where a finger or a toe should be. The head wound was really the worst part. Just freaking disgusting the wound was. It looked like they put a hammer right through the skull a few times; you could see brains. I've never seen brains before, although I watched a few zombie movies where the zombie eats brains. But those are fake brains, even though now I know they actually look just like real brains. The special effects are amazing in these modern movies, huh? But you want to know the most interesting part, Sheriff?"

"No, I was hoping you'd keep the most interesting part to yourself."

"The most interesting part is I didn't throw up. I started to a little in the mouth, but I held it. Pretty good, huh? Doctor Chloe says it was because of all this violence we experience on the job. She called it *desensitization*. Not sure what that means, but the state police guys didn't agree with her. They said it was because I was plenty dense. Just sour grapes if you ask me, Sheriff. I took twenty bucks off each and every one of those state suckers," said Deputy Drew proudly.

Gus took his hat off and saluted Drew with it. "You are a credit to my staff, and don't let anyone tell you different. Not that you'd understand them if they did insult you. By the way, did you happen to catch the name of the girl, so I know which of the missing girls the dead body was?"

"Doctor Chloe said her name was Pam Martin. They took the body away to the coroner's, and the state boys then went up to the ranch to question the ranch hands. They said they were probably prime suspects and we were too stupid to realize it. One of them is probably an illegal and a sex maniac to boot. They must have been impressed by us locals, because while they were gone investigating the ranch hands they left me in charge of the whole crime scene. They told me to wait here and keep an eye on the investigation scene until they got back. So that's what I been doing. Well, that and calling you to make sure you knew what was going on. I wouldn't want you missing out on anything."

Gus looked out over the investigation scene. There was no scene anymore. The site was clear of people, bodies, and clues. This killer didn't leave much unintentionally behind last time, and Gus doubted he suddenly made a mistake. The whole area was abandoned except for a small calf in the distance. The calf had an unimpressed look on its face. Gus could imagine it thinking, There are two sad, clueless idiots. Gus didn't argue with the calf for fear it would just validate the point.

So the state police had frozen Gus out of his own investigation. The whole awful mess started out as Gus's investigation, and had the victims been poor, ugly daughters of the rural county, he would probably have had to beg for any state help on the case. They wouldn't have given a damn, and Gus would be not only be in the loop but at the top of it. Instead the victims turned out to be beautiful daughters of people deemed to matter to society, so now it was their people's investigation.

Well, thought Gus, let them talked to Ernie's men all they want. They'll probably get a few cases for the immigration people, but they won't find a murderer, unless they frame one for the crime. The state police weren't above framing a person for a crime. Gus wasn't above it either, come to think of it. But he wanted to at least feel he knew which local people were worth framing for a crime. In the old days that's what they all did, but times were changing fast, and the job was getting harder.

"Drew, you keep an eye on the vehicles while I look over the crime scene," said Gus, saluting the deputy with his hat.

"I will, Sheriff."

Gus wandered from the edge of the roadside once more into Ernie's ranch. He came up to the fence where he had fallen off and tweaked his back. He leaned against the fence and looked down on the other side. There was the yellow tape blowing gently in the dry heat of the day. The ground was pressed down where Gus assumed the second body had lain. The area was matted down from the feet of countless people around the investigation scene. It was approximately where the first body was, so that suggested it was the same murderer. It was a good spot to dump a body at night. So good they had done it twice without so much as a good witness. But anyone who read the past week's newspaper stories could have known the location of the first body.

There was no smoking gun laying in plain view to tell Gus who did this. Gus didn't expect to see one. Gus was looking at the investigation scene for one reason only: he wanted to see how much blood was on the ground. You don't bash someone's head in to the point it leaks brains and not generate a bloody mess. There was no bloody mess here, and that could only mean one thing to every investigator involved: the young woman was killed someplace else.

You couldn't tell at first glance that the first body was even dead. That first girl could have died anywhere but probably wasn't killed here either. But this time it was definite that the girl wasn't killed here. Everyone else already knew what Gus just found out, and yet they still went off to talk to Ernie's men. Either they're idiots or they're looking for a fast and easy decision. Sheriff Gus now felt he knew about all there was to know here too, and he also knew it was never going to do any good to talk to those men at the ranch. For the first murder it had been a good hunch they weren't worth the time to talk to, and the second murder just proved him right. An

94

accidental death might involve the ranch hands, but a brutal torture and murder…what would be the point?

Gus continued to lean on the fence and watch his calf friend in the distance. The calf continued to watch him. He tried in his mind to reason with the calf to let loose what information it knew. It went to figure that a nosy cow like that knew something about two dead girls.

The young women were friends with each other. They were last seen alive in the company of each other. They were now both found dead in the same approximate location, a few days apart. That was the end of the similarities in the case. One girl's neck was broken, and she had possibly died of complications of a drug overdose. This new dead girl was tortured and beaten. She had died a horrible and cruel death. The first one could have been an accident; this one could never have been an accident.

The crimes didn't fit together. Sure, the same party that panicked and dumped the first body could have killed the other girl to get rid of a witness—but they hadn't really panicked the first time. They had cleaned that first body of all useful evidence. There's not much panic if you wait days to kill the next victim. Little calf, he thought, it doesn't make sense to old Sheriff Gus.

The calf kept his distance and chewed on cud while he watched Gus lean on the fence. He was going to have to make a next move if he was going to stay ahead of the other players in the investigation. He could take the easy way out and frame up someone as your basic sex maniac that kills young women. It made perfect sense, and the county was bound to believe it to be true. You have a sex maniac murderer that killed two attractive girls. He killed one accidentally, panicked, and dumped the body (yet in a non-panicked and controlled fashion). The second girl was a witness maybe, and she died a cold-hearted, slow death of teeth pulling, finger smashing, and eventual bashing in of the head.

But if you wanted to silence a witness, why not just strangle her? Why mutilate her? The blood alone was going to be all over where you did the murder. She might not be a witness anymore, but the mess left behind from killing her that way would tell a bad tale against you anyways.

Worst of all was the drugs. Who put the drugs on the first body? He was pretty sure Dr. Armstrong would never have missed them on that first day. Why have a perfectly clean murder and then go to the trouble to break into the coroner's office and add evidence, evidence that actually led Gus to someone in the county that saw you, the likely murderer? So, while you could frame someone as a sex murderer easy enough, once you went over what was going on, it sure felt like it was going to take a lot to get all that to make sense to a jury.

Gus wondered where the last missing girl was right now. You don't silence one witness and leave the other alive. Did that mean the last girl was involved somehow? It didn't seem likely, as these party girls were all pretty much the same, weren't they? Disposable pretty girls; just bad luck who of them died first, and perhaps random chance who was dead next. Gus tried to imagine Mandy Henderson bashing someone's head in with a hammer. Pretty party girls don't bash each other in the head with hammers and dump bodies in fields. At least not nice girls from the neighborhoods these girls were from. So if she was still alive for the moment, it wasn't because she was in on the thing. No, if she was still alive, it was due to random good luck. And these girls were now dead from random bad luck.

Gus looked out into the ranch. The little calf was bending down, taking in another mouthful. It lifted his head up and stared at Gus. The calf was just another dumb witness. A silent spy that had his information locked where no human could reach it. There was one last young woman out there that would benefit from that info, but there's some information that is likely never going to be available. The little calf kept his secrets better than any human.

Gus left his fence and headed back up toward the roadside. Gus glanced down the road to examine the Lance Daniels billboard glaring down on him.

"This job sucks more days than not, Lance my friend. Don't go fooling yourself," Gus said out loud. He walked up over to Drew standing guard to the empty road.

"Drew, you don't vote, do you?"

"Nah, I never have. Never saw a use in voting anyways. If you vote and your guy loses, then you feel like a loser. If you vote and your guy wins and does a bad job, you feel like it is your fault. If you vote, your guy wins, and he does a good job, then no one ever gives you any credit. Voting is for suckers."

"I knew there must be something I liked about you, boy."

"Anyways, they say we convicted felons aren't allowed to vote in this state."

"Aren't felons generally not allowed to be officers in the sheriff's department either?"

Drew scratched the top of his head. "I don't know, sheriff. Knowing the law was never one of my strong suits. My daddy always said a man should perspire to their natural position in life."

"Well, he found you a perfectly natural job for someone that doesn't know the law but is often in trouble with it. Well, I'll leave you in charge of here. This is one place I'm sure you can manage to keep up the good work and improve the department's image."

Gus climbed back into the sheriff's truck. He popped open the glove compartment and looked over the manila envelope that contained the case file. He pulled out the fax with the plate numbers from the college. He then dug into his pockets for the paper he received from Trash Tannehill. He compared the two. Toward the middle of page 2 of the fax he found a match. It was the same plate that Trash saw, but according to the computer it belonged to a red van and not a black car (or a blue Mercedes). It was the same plate, but somehow someone registered it to a totally fictitious car. Either that or someone stole someone else's license plates, and the campus parking police didn't actually write down the makes and models of the cars in the lots, they just wrote down plate numbers and looked up the corresponding vehicles in some database. Was it a red van that showed up at the girls' dorm, or was it a blue Mercedes with a red van's plates? Well, it had been over a week; someone would have reported stolen plates by now.

Gus picked up the police radio and called up the station. He ran off the plate number as well as the plate numbers around it on the fax. At least he'd find out which company Tannehill was talking about that owned these cars. If they were reported stolen, he'd find that out too. He probably should have looked for stolen plates among the list already. He thought the state boys would have figured out to do that by now. He felt he was slipping further behind, taking with him his chances of remaining sheriff.

Gus placed the piece of paper and the fax back into the manila folder and decided he'd head back to the office. With any luck the plates would be ready by the time he arrived. Had he fronted the expense, he could have had one of those computer things installed in the sheriff truck and he'd have all the information right here and now. But until right now Gus had never really wanted more computer technology around him.

Just then the most dreaded of all computer technology went off. Gus's cell phone both buzzed and bleeped a stale tone over and over again. Gus looked at the screen to see if it was someone he wanted to talk to. Not likely, as that was a very short list.

Gus pushed a button, and with a beep Terrance was on the phone talking.

"Where are you? It's only two hours until the big debate."

"Is that tonight?"

"How can you forget the big debate's date? You haven't also forgotten the big debate's location, have you? It's at the charter school auditorium in the development. Are you familiar with the charter school in the development?"

"I sure am, Terrance. The principal and I are old friends. You just wait there and take it easy. I'll be there as soon as I can."

There wasn't anything left to do here anyway. Yet a terrible thought came over Gus: What if they come back a third time? He'd station Deputy Drew here for the next week if he had to. If they came back, they'd be out of missing persons to find. Maybe Drew would catch the murderer, but Gus didn't think he'd get that lucky.

Gus turned on the radio while driving over to the school for the debate. Gus was hoping to hear what information the radio had on the case. Mostly they were talking about unidentified sources that told them the state police were about to arrest a person of interest for the murders. The arrest was imminent, according to the news. Gus wasn't sure what *imminent* meant, but he was pretty sure it didn't mean *totally imaginary*.

They claimed the station's source had given them the suspect's name, and they were going to reveal it just after another commercial break. Gus listened through three commercial breaks. No names or arrests were ever revealed. It was an old game of how to keep an idiot in suspense: "I'll tell you later..." Once it was just a funny joke for four-year-olds to tell each other; now it was the entire philosophical basis for the broadcast news media industry. Gus finally turned the radio off. Perhaps they changed the meaning of the word *imminent* after all.

Gus's truck pulled into the charter school parking lot. The lot was lightly filled. Debates between two candidates for sheriff weren't exactly a hot ticket, even if the tickets were free. Gus parked his truck next to a silver car. He paused to look it over to see if it was the same one that had tailed him earlier. Gus wasn't sure one way or another. It could be, as so many cars looked alike these days. He looked around the lot for black cars or a blue Mercedes. There were three black cars, but none matched the plate number in the manila envelope. There was no blue Mercedes in the lot. Life wasn't that easy, and murderers apparently weren't big debate fans.

He was almost inside the building when he stopped in his tracks and went back to the sheriff truck. He opened the passenger seat and looked for his hat. He found it on the floor. With a forlorn look, Gus put the hat on and tried to straighten the brim in the truck's side mirror. He looked like an idiot, but that was the part he was supposed to play.

Terrance was waiting for him just outside the entrance. "Gus, you are cutting it close. Make sure to read these index cards over real quick. I've made some important notes for you on the agreed-upon debate topics."

Gus reluctantly glanced at the pile of index cards. "Could you give me a brief summary, because I can guarantee you I'm not exactly in the mood to read a bunch of pointless political mumbo jumbo."

"Look, we took a survey of the likely voter crowd. The survey company used likely voter profiled information to give us an estimate of the mood of the audience tonight. We expect a social-libertarian crowd that leans toward authoritarian conservatism when dealing with economic issues and toward democratic socialism on domestic-spending issues."

Gus dropped the index cards on the ground. "OK, I give up. What does any of that mean? And don't tell me not to worry cause it's covered in the cards."

"Don't worry, Gus, they mean nothing at all. They're just words. While those terms certainly have classical formal definitions in a political-science classroom and mountains of philosophy books written to bore a reader for hours, thanks to our modern politicians the words have lost any logical meaning. The point of these labels is not to know what they mean but to know that the crowd thinks they mean something and have bothered to self-identify as these things on our surveys. Thus what is important is not what they might mean to some Ivy League professor, Gus, it is what Joe Six-Pack thinks they mean. Since Joe Six-Pack doesn't really know, your job is to convince them the words mean what they want them to mean. Do you get my meaning, Gus?"

"Well, what does the crowd think they mean? And once again please don't tell me that it is on the cards."

"Our profiling assures us this crowd doesn't think much. Just try to tell them what they want to hear. Leave it good and vague and allow the audience to fill in the meaning themselves. If they like you, they will more than oblige you by pretending whatever they wanted you to say is what they thought you said. If they hate you, then any word or phrase, no matter how innocent, will sound to them like you are quoting Hitler."

"Well, I don't speak German, so I think we might be in good shape"

"Oh, one more thing that is on those card: it is a town hall meeting, so the questions will come from the voters themselves." Terrance looked down at his watch. "Crap, Gus, you better get in there."

Gus wandered into the auditorium. The small crowd was mostly white. The longtime residents from the county were not well represented by the crowd. No doubt this was because the debate was being held in the development. Marty was sitting in the front row with a pad, waiting to take down notes; well, at least this embarrassing performance would be well documented in the paper. Next to him was sitting a very beautiful woman and two lovely kids. Gus assumed this was Lance's lovely wife and kids. Gus looked around to make sure none of his relatives were in the crowd. The last thing he needed was his daughter or any of his wife's family showing up. He figured the crowd was already going to be hostile enough; he didn't need anyone that personally knew him to stir it up more. His daughter had argued with him to leave the sheriff's office for years. She claimed the job was less than perfectly moral. Morality was one of those things you got to argue about when someone else paid your tuition fees.

The moderator motioned him up onto the stage. She talked through the debate rules. Gus vaguely paid attention to the moderator, as he spent majority of the time examining his opponent. His clothes were real, but his mannerisms left Gus feeling the man was a fake from head to toe. His appearance was that of a man built of the doll parts Gus used to step on in the middle of the night when his daughter had been young. The guy's hair was too good, his teeth were too white, and his clothes were too spotless. Gus wondered to himself once again why anyone like this would ever want his job. If that was the look of all the future sheriffs of this country, then the Trash Tannehills of the world were in for one soft ride. (Technically it was a soft ride already for them, but as a matter of principle Gus thought somehow this guy would find a way to make it softer.)

A buzzer went off and snapped Gus out of his temporary daydream. He hoped the rules didn't matter anymore than all of Terrance's research. Either way he hadn't listened to either the rules or what Terrance was trying to explain. There was now a second dead girl and Gus still had no clue who had killed either of them or why. All he knew was that the whole thing made no sense, but it had to make sense. Someone killed them and it sure didn't seem like a sex maniac. Another buzzer went off, and Lance bounded to the front of the stage. Gus didn't know if they were going out together or one at a time. Did it matter? Screw it all, thought Gus, and he wandered out to the podiums on the stage as well. Lance moved toward him to shake his hand. Lance gave him one of those fade-away jerk handshakes. Gus disliked him and he didn't even know the man.

The moderator said, "We have provided microphones throughout the audience for your questions. Lance Daniels won the coin toss and will get our first question."

Gus saw an old white-haired lady moving toward a microphone. He settled himself firmly behind his podium. The high school stage lights blared down on him, and that combined with the stupid hat made his head uncomfortably warm.

The old woman had a surprisingly strong speaking voice and boomed out the first question. "I hate this whole daylight savings time. I swear half the time I can't remember if I'm springing forward or falling back. Why do the communists in our government screw around with my American time?"

Lance confidentially moved up to the microphone on his podium. He spoke in a controlled rhythmic voice. "This is a great question and I am glad this issue has been brought up in tonight's debate. The issue we have at hand is daylight savings, my friends. I ask you, what is daylight savings actually trying to save you from? I'll tell you what it is trying to save you from. It is trying to save you from Europeanism! I think it is time for America to turn away from this law based on an English concept of time. For a brief moment each year, daylight savings frees us all from the binds of European time slavery that holds us at the mercy of our previous colonial master, but it is not enough! Our forefathers fought for freedom from the British Empire to create the single greatest nation on Earth. America! Why should we forfeit their hard-fought victory? The left-wing socialist radical Woodrow Wilson passed time laws that tied our beautiful nation down to a time based in Greenwich, England. I repeat: Greenwich is in England. They did this even after our great nation stuck a boot in kind King George's behind to gain the precious freedom we all enjoy today. These Tory lovers want us to use Greenwich Mean Time. That the word *mean* is in the name is no accident, my friends, because as we all know the English are mean and desperate to take over our country with Europeanism. I will not force upon my fellow countrymen a European, socialized unit of time-centric zones. It is about time we had a person in charge that puts America back on American time!"

102

The old woman that asked the question wiped a tear from her eye and began to clap softly. The crowd responded with a clap that crawled through the audience. The momentum grew until there were cheers and hoots directed at the stage. Finally someone in the audience clearly yelled out, "'Merica!"

The moderator then took control of the crowd. "Sheriff, you have two minutes to respond."

"Uh…I'm not the sharpest cookie in the drawer, but I'm pretty sure the sheriff's office is not in charge of daylight saving enforcement. I can't and won't arrest you for not observing time in Greenwich fashion or any fashion. I don't even know where Greenwich is. I suggest that your concerns about daylight savings are not a law-enforcement issue that I or any elected sheriff can help you with."

The crowd shifted uneasy in their seats. The old lady looked confused. A murmur of "he doesn't even know the law" traveled from one person to another person that didn't know the law.

The moderator rapidly spoke up to keep the murmur in check by asking for the next question; this time Gus would answer first.

A dapper-looking young man in glasses came to the microphone. "For years this country has been drowning in partisan politics. What will you do to end the political stalemate and turn this country towards a more bipartisan future?" The audience clapped at the question.

Gus stood up straight next to the microphone. He cleared his throat and began to speak. "As I am sure you all know, the position of sheriff is a non-partisan office in this county."

The room sat in dead silence for a good minute. The warmth was getting to Gus's head and sweat started to bead up on his forehead. The awkward silence wasn't doing much for his confidence—not that he had much in the first place. Only two questions in, and it was pretty clear to Gus he had lost control of the debate. Finally, to Gus's relief, the silence was broken.

"Lance Daniels, you have two minutes to respond."

"I am glad these fine citizens have all come here tonight to bring these important issues to the front of this critical election. The lying partisan media ignores what is on the hearts and minds of the public and focuses instead on non-relevant political posturing. I agree, far too often partisan politicians like my opponent here let party stand in front of policy. I guarantee you, the bipartisan voting public, that I will use my bipartisan position to reach across the aisle to form solid nonpartisan agreements that will move this partisan present towards a postpartisan future, where my bipartisan position will dissolve into a neo-postpartisan position centered on you the voter's unmoving, heavily partisan hearts."

The crowd once again cheered, and there may have been a few marriage proposals shouted at the stage. Gus couldn't be sure, because he was busy clearing the sweat from his brow. The moderator interrupted the Lance love-fest in the auditorium to get the next question up to the microphone. A middle-aged voter in a cheap three-piece suit came up to the microphone. Standing next to him was his artificial-looking plastic wife in a horrible flower-print dress.

The man spoke. "As sheriff, what are you going to do in these public schools to educate my kids so my children will keep off of the drugs?"

It was again Lance's turn to answer first. He smiled in reassuring fashion. "This is yet another on-the-mark point brought to this thought-provoking community event. I think all of us here tonight understand that this county is split between those living by traditional American family values, the soul of this national Judeo-Christian-based republican democracy, and the new illegal, foreign, criminal elements moving into our pleasant community. Far too often the previous sheriff has allowed new carpetbaggers that carry non-traditional American values into our school system to corrupt this honest community. I say it is time to return America back to Americans. We do not need to compromise our America to outsiders and their criminal drug habits. I assure you I will keep our communities' streets, schools, churches, and synagogues drug dealer free. I dare say I will charter our schools to a new drug-free future. I will create in the charter schools a proactive educational and instructional program designed to keep your kids off drugs and away from the foreign theme of the new, dirty, one-world street idealism."

This was apparently exactly what the man asking the question wanted to hear. He nodded in affirmation throughout Lance's response. As far as Gus could tell, Lance just told the man that all the drug problems were minorities' fault and that Lance was going to crack down on non-whites. The irony to Gus was these new development people were the carpetbaggers, not the Mexicans and rednecks who had lived in the county for generations. The nerve of these people, cheering for soft, cowardly racism! If the audience wasn't tolerant, then Gus decided he had run out of tolerance for the debate as well.

"Sheriff Gus, you will have two minutes to respond."

Gus sighed and looked over the audience. The audience glared back at Gus with unhappy little faces.

"Look, I'm running to be your sheriff, not your school teacher. If you want your kids all educated and not stupid, I suggest that you be that way yourself. Don't go all running and crying to Sheriff Gus because your kid is smoking crack and turning tricks when you spent every day while raising them smoking weed and cracking open six packs. Kids aren't as stupid as you think. If they see you disrespect the drug laws and your body, then they will grow up to do stupid stuff with drugs themselves. Stop blaming the schools for the fact you have never read a book to your kid and never sat down and went over their homework. Sheriff Gus can put on a Rusty the Meth-Hating Dog suit and tell them little darlings all Gus's drug horror stories he's seen over the years, but that won't make a lick of difference if you're all a bunch of stupid fucks at home."

The audience shifted uneasily. Several items appeared to be tossed at the stage in the direction of Gus. The moderator quickly took over the situation and ushered in the next questioner to the microphone.

An overweight middle-aged woman in a trendy yoga outfit stepped up to the microphone. "The local government is dragging down the county's economy. When is this county going to stop pouring tax money into this bigger-government nanny state and get that money to our job creators like myself?"

It was Gus's turn to speak first, but Lance beat Gus to the draw. "This audience is one of the most inspiring audiences I have ever talked to. You effervesce tonight with the pulse of the American entrepreneurial spirit. I can only hope your children at home understand how much each and every one of you loves this country. I think you can see the true color of my opponent. I tell you, we good American politicians are not like needles in a haystack. You are good honest people, and I trust you know a liar from a man like me, who tells you the cold hard facts. For too long the sheriff office has impeded the growth of the American capitalist spirit. I assure you, I will not allow our jobs to be taken by illegal people, illegal trade, and illegal welfare. I promise that those that work hard and honest have nothing to fear from this man"—he pointed to himself—"but trust me, they have plenty to fear from my opponent. My opponent has spent years on the big government's dime and protecting the big government's interests, and all on your private tax dollars. So I repeat: if you want to see job creators get a fair shake, it is time to shake up the big government and turn a private citizen like myself toward these public offices."

The crowd ate it up again. The moderator turned to Sheriff Gus for his response.

Gus leaned uneasily on the podium. The microphone hissed momentarily with a crack of feedback. Gus then said, "There is nothing in the sheriff's job description that says I'm a job creator. I don't even know what that term means. You people have some nerve blaming me and the government for your lack of job creation. Hell, most of you don't even work in this county. You work in the city, buy your goods in the city, and then come into our county because it is the only place you can afford a house. Meanwhile the long-term county residents are the ones without jobs. If you stupid fucking people go voting time and time again for people that think handing our tax dollars to privatized companies that charge more than the government to do basic service while shipping your jobs overseas is the solution to unemployment and lower crime, then that's your fault, not good old Sheriff Gus's. It also isn't Sheriff Gus that is cutting social security, school programs, and welfare, all of which makes crime the only way some folks can possibly make money to earn a living. If you want less crime, stop blaming me for you voting like a bunch of idiots. Stop pointing your fingers at me in the government when it's you

106

stupid fucking voters that enable the empty suits like my opponent to make your lives worse."

The audience openly booed. Several threats to step outside and fight it out could be heard. Gus, on the other hand, smiled for the first time that night. If you were going to lose, you might as well lose with the truth.

Gus put his hat on and headed out the auditorium door. Terrance, cell phone pressed to his ear, stopped him before he got out of the exit. "Yeah, mayor, I got our star debater right here." Terrance turned to Gus and put his hand over the cell phone to mute it. "Gus, the mayor is super excited about the debate tonight. He was watching it on local-access TV. He wants to have a congratulatory word with you." Terrance handed over his cell phone to Gus.

The mayor's voice spoke out of the cell phone. "Gus, that was an amazing performance, the best debate performance I think I've ever witnessed. That little out-of-towner prick was standing all dapper and dandy, and there you were giving him the what for. I could see the anger and the spirit in your body. You had the working man's sweat coming out of you, while your opponent looked like a man that never did a day's work. I can assure you, that performance made the county proud tonight, Gus!"

"Did you happen to have your TV's sound on?"

"No, I'm a busy man. I don't have time to both watch and listen, you understand. But you looked fantastic."

Gus tossed the phone back to Terrance and placed the cowboy hat on his handler's head. "The mayor loved it. Three more years for sure." Gus laughed and headed out the door.

Gus made it back to the sheriff truck and noticed the silver car was gone. His passenger window was smashed in, glass all over the seat. His glove compartment was open and his manila folder was gone. Well, he thought, that officially cemented the debate as a disaster. Gus closed the passenger door and went to the driver's side and climbed in.

It wasn't a complete loss. Lance said a little something that had struck an idea in Gus's head: the needle in the haystack reference. Gus had been finding dead, rich, beautiful girls because they stuck out like sore thumbs in the middle of ranch land. People like Trash left their dead bodies buried out in the desert where no one would find them. Gus was looking for a good-looking man that could attract rich girls from the city college. Where in the county was a rich, young, good-looking guy like a needle in a haystack? A blue, limited-edition Mercedes would stick out anywhere in this county except one place: right here in the development. Right here a guy like the one he was searching for was cloaked by just standing out in the open. Now all Gus had to find was someone that knew the development like the back of his hand but wasn't part of the development, someone that would notice things because they didn't belong. But who was that?

CHAPTER 5

Gus woke up on his sofa in pain. He had wanted to purchase a couch, but his wife insisted on buying a sofa for the living room. Frankly, to this day Gus did not understand the difference between the two articles of furniture. He did understand that falling asleep on the sofa was usually terrible for his general overall health.

Unfortunately he had had trouble falling asleep after the debate. He was still mad at himself for allowing those two press agents to get their hands on his entire folder of information on the case. His plan to starve them of information hadn't worked out any better than his debate performance. If they made interesting news items from the papers inside, Marty would be calling him to complain about being scooped. Still, that wasn't really why Gus got up from his bed and wandered over to the sofa in the middle of the night.

Nor was it the debate. It hadn't gone all that well, but his side seemed to have liked it. Even his eighty-nine-year-old Aunt Elma called and left a message on his home answering machine to tell him she was glad to hear someone finally stick it to those development people. That coupled with the mayor's praise seemed to reaffirm that debate performances were in the eye of the beholder.

Gus tried to remember the scenario that resulted in him having to sleep on the sofa. He seemed to remember around three in the morning drinking a cup of gin and mulling the murder case over and over in his head. He had to settle for a paper cup of gin, because he couldn't find any glasses proper for drinking gin. He had shot glasses somewhere in the house, but he hadn't bothered with them since his wife died. With no one around he could drink straight out of the bottle if he chose to and no one was left to complain. Now, in the morning, he couldn't remember why suddenly he'd used a paper cup. More importantly, he couldn't think of how to find his lost needle in the haystack of the development. That is, until about three solid cups of gin were in him, and then suddenly the debate and the reporters sort of merged, and he formed a plan.

He picked up the dry paper cup that he had accidentally fallen asleep on. The gin-induced plan was slowly coming back to him. First thing's first, though. He took a shower, had a shave, and dressed in his cleanest uniform. Then he went over to the phone.

Three rings on the phone and Marty picked up. "I hope you aren't calling me complaining about the article on the debate coverage."

Gus replied. "I haven't even read the morning paper, but I can imagine what it says. I called because I got another favor to ask of you."

"Look, Gus, I'm busy. I can't do more free investigating for you without a scoop. I need to keep delivering a killer of a story to my readers if I want to stay in business."

"Well, I think your competitors out-scooped you last night, because someone hit my truck post-debate and stole information important to the case."

"You know which paper or station these competitors work for? If they got something good, they haven't released it. I've been tracking the dailies and the stations. Nothing new since yesterday's body. Local Sheriff robbed! At least the locals would be interested. I don't need anything super juicy; between this new murder and the daily check from Sigmund Smudge to print his editorial, this paper is actually in the black for once. Sorry about those smear editorials, but you know I wouldn't keep printing them if so many damn readers weren't asking for them. I'd give him a full-time editorial position in the paper if the guy would just give me a return address. People do love a poison pen pal."

"Yeah, yeah, I'm sure you're all broken up about it. Business is business and so on. Look, I called on another matter altogether, and it is an urgent law-enforcement matter. I need to know who your delivery boys are in the development. All of them."

"I'm going to reply with the ultimate of questions first before I just reply to that request: what for?"

"If it pans out as anything, I promise I'll tell you. It will be a genuine scoop just for you, Marty."

"Look, Gus, when I said I need to deliver a killer story to my readers, I didn't mean my stories were delivered by killers. Do you think a delivery boy did those murders? I can't see that as very likely. Not with all the information I've read and printed in the news," pointed out Marty.

"I ain't saying yes or no to any questions as of this morning. I just want the names. I gave you a little scoop about the truck break-in, so now give me a little scoop back."

"Well, for starters, Gus, there aren't any delivery boys or girls these days. That went out years ago. We got a small independent firm that does all the transport and delivering for the paper. They got their own fleet of vans and do it for us and the city papers too. Most people in the development get the city paper, not the local paper. I think we both know why. Still, we do have mild circulation in the development. I've got an application for those online mobile things that lets a subscriber read paper stories free if they're paying customers. That helps boost sales in the development. Since you promised me a possible big scoop, I'll give you the address for the delivery company. As an added bonus I'll give you a little good news and a little bad news. The bad news is I didn't find any story based on that Internet porn tip you gave me. The good news is something I haven't worked out whether it's worth a story or not yet: my sources tell me the money for Lance Daniels is coming from something called the McGruffin Corporation. I looked up the company, but it has zero ties to this area. Not that there is much information on this company at all. It's interesting, but at the moment not interesting enough to sell a bunch of papers and Internet ads. Does that name mean anything to you Gus?"

Gus paused. "Nope, but it might later on."

"Later on after what?"

"I don't know, but if I find out, you'll be the first person I think of to tell."

And with that Gus hung up the phone. Good ol' Marty came through with the Lance Daniels money question after all. It was a bit of disappointing news, though. Gus had hoped the money came from the drug gangs or something even seedier. True, no one in the rural town liked a faceless corporation run by CEO bastards, but ultimately Gus agreed with Marty about the interest level of the news. That particular story wasn't juicy enough yet to get much of a bite.

Gus was on the move again, driving out to the address of the newspaper distribution company. It was in the middle of the old industrial heart of the county, which was now mostly empty red brick buildings. Some of the buildings were repurposed into self-storage centers. Gus's destination was a building on the main interstate route that also led up eventually to the highway. Not a bad location at all for this type of business. The building looked heavily beat up by the passing of years but still fresh compared to the small fleet of whitish vans that read Newspapers on the sides. The vans also had a phone number to call for information on getting home delivery, but the grime on the back made reading any of the numbers a difficult task.

Gus drove the sheriff truck into the loading dock at the back of the building. On the loading dock were a group of men sitting around in several small groups. Apparently they had mostly finished their work for the day, after the very early morning deliveries. Some of them were eating lunch, some of them were playing cards, and some appeared to be playing on electronic devices. But all of them stopped whatever they had been doing and had their eyes fixed at the sheriff truck as soon as it arrived at the loading dock.

Painfully aware of the faces eyeing him with suspicion, Gus climbed out of the truck in as friendly a manner as he could muster. He waved a friendly hello and faked a silly grin on his face. "Hello, I was wondering if you fellows could possibly help the sheriff's department out with a little information."

"Hey, man, we didn't do nothing!" shouted an older man sitting on the dock. "We are good, hard-working citizens, and we do nothing you would be interested in. You got no right to come here and act like we're doing something here."

Gus had a guess that he was either the owner or the foreman of this group. All Gus wanted was a little help, but to get it he would have to play the good cop. It was going to be tough sell to these men, because the sheriff's department over the years had built a much-deserved bad-cop reputation, particularly to the kind of people that could afford to live off delivering newspapers. Gus approached the old man cautiously and tried to keep up friendly appearances.

"I'm looking for the guys that deliver newspapers to the development."

The old man now approached him. "Why you need to know which of us work where? Those guys have done nothing to those people in the development but work hard for them. Unless you got papers telling us we need to talk to you, then you go away right now. We got nothing to tell you, because we all have done nothing."

"I didn't say any of you did anything. It's you that keeps bringing up what you have and haven't done. I'm only here because I happen to be looking for a car. It is a really nice blue Mercedes. It probably would be very polished, well-kept, and detailed regularly. I believe this car is now at some house somewhere in the development."

The old man made a shooing motion at Gus. "You'll waste your time speaking here with us. We didn't steal this precious car. We are not thieves! This is my company, and I resent you telling me I hire thieves!"

"I didn't say it was stolen. It hasn't been stolen, as far as I know. For the moment all I know for sure is that I am looking for it. After I find it, then I can tell if it has been stolen or not. What it really comes down to is this: I am really looking for the location of the house where the car was last seen. I have a great interest in information on the occupants of that house. And so I need to know if someone has seen that car. I've been told your men know that area very well. I could drive the neighborhood for days, but your men have been driving that whole area every single day for weeks and years. So I'm figuring your men might have noticed a really nice car like this."

"You wait here," said the old man. The men now gathered together in a tight group far away from Gus. They spoke in Spanish to each other. Gus had lived around Spanish speakers his whole life yet never bothered to learn a word of the language, and in brief moments like this he regretted it.

The owner spoke again. "We don't deliver to any houses with that kind of car."

Gus replied, "It might not be at a house you deliver to, but my gut tells me it is in the development."

Now another man finally spoke up. "I know that car. It is at fifty-four Sandia Road. It is a really nice car, heavily modified. The kind of car you don't forget when you see it. I deliver a paper to the house two doors down. I even went to this house one time to ask if they wanted the paper. Really it was just to look at the car up close. But I didn't do anything wrong or touch their car or nothing; I just looked at it. If this man says I touched it, then he is a liar."

"So it was a man at the house. What kind of man was he? Could you describe him?"

"I don't remember. He looked nice and expensive. Too nice-looking for the development even. I also remember he was very rude to me. He called me a leech and told me real people read their news online. Real people don't kill the trees to read government-reduced bullshit, mass pro-duced for the idiots like myself. I remember exactly his words, so you see I am not as stupid as this man thinks. I admit he did make me very angry, so as I left his house I spit on the car. I swear that is all I did, though."

Gus tipped his hat to the man. "I believe you, son. And don't worry; as far as I am concerned, this car matter is officially closed. I have a feeling no one in this county is going to like the man that owns that car very much. The sheriff's office thanks you for your help. You boys go ahead and have yourselves a good day."

Gus turned and headed back to the truck. The men shrugged to each other at the lack of an incident. They had expected trouble. Perhaps they still did. They all stared in disbelief as Gus started up the truck and slowly backed out onto the road. When Gus was out of sight the old man turned to his men.

"A sex maniac is terrorizing our women one by one, and all that sheriff is interested in is fancy automobiles." The men grumbled and returned to their afternoon off-time.

Gus was looking in vain for Sandia Road. Quickly built houses in six different bland styles lined the road. The houses came in ten varieties of color. Many of the houses had fake brick or stucco exteriors as well. After a while Gus found himself becoming road blind from staring at the exact same house over and over again throughout the development.

Gus generally avoided calls to the development if he could. The calls were pretty much always domestic disputes. There was little Gus or any officer could do to prevent two people who couldn't stand each other but remained with each other from beating each other up over and over, particularly when they were very drunk. The problem houses in the development were known to all the deputies in the department within six months of being hired. It was using this vague map that Gus found his way to Sandia Road.

The sheriff truck passed the number 54 and headed a few blocks beyond before making its way back around for a second pass. It was a quick scouting trip to see if a car of any kind was out front of the residence. There was no car in the driveway or along the side of the curbless road. On the second go past the house, Gus slowed the truck and pulled it into the driveway across the street. He went up to the front door of number 53 and rang the doorbell. A small child answered the door by opening it up just a crack.

"What you want?"

Gus bent over as best he could to get at eye level with the child. His back still ached from the night on the sofa. "Well, hello there, little partner. I want to speak with your daddy or your mommy. Now you be a good lad and just run off to fetch one of them for good old Sheriff Gus."

"Can't," replied the child.

Gus held his badge up to the crack in the door to see if that helped matters. "Why can't you help me, little partner?"

"Ain't home," said the child rapidly in response.

Gus began to worry that a child endangerment case was about to halt his investigation. "You mean your parents left you home all alone?"

"Nope!" boomed the voice through the crack.

"So there is an adult presence looking out for you. Could this adult perhaps come to the door and speak to old Gus, the local sheriff?"

"Nope! There's no adult, just my stupid sister is here."

Well, progress at last, thought Gus. And the case of child endangerment was, to his relief, getting less likely. "Can I speak with her? It's an urgent matter."

"Nope!"

Frustrated, Gus rather bluntly and rudely returned a reply. "Well, why on Earth can't I?"

"Sleeping! Do you want to know a secret?" asked the boy, now suddenly whispering.

Gus whispered back, "I suppose so."

"When my momma goes out and leaves me and my sister alone, my sister drinks my daddy's beer. My sister thinks Momma doesn't know." The boy stopped and looked around to make sure he and the sheriff were alone at the door. Satisfied his sister wasn't around, he continued, "But Momma knows. I think she's gonna get a whippin' tonight for sure," replied the boy, ending the comment in rather eager fashion.

Gus's plan wasn't off to a great start, but he worked with what he had. "You're a nosy little partner, ain't you? What I mean by that is that you sound like a good kid that likes to know about things. Sheriff Gus here thinks maybe you're the kind of good kid that snoops around the neighborhood and does a little investigating. There's a lot of information floating around a neighborhood a little boy good at investigating can find out. I bet you find out all kinds of things that people don't think you know."

The child nodded his head in affirmation.

Gus pulled out a folded picture of a blue Mercedes from his pocket. "Good. I knew I could count on you. Have you in all your stealthy investigating ever seen a car like this in your neighbor's driveway?" Gus shoved the picture through the crack in the door.

The child reached his hand out through the door crack and snatched the picture. He made sounds on the other side of the door that would indicate he was getting excited. His head reappeared in the door crack and he nodded yes.

"Was the neighbor that had this car the one just there across the street?"

"Yip, sir, that was the house, but it ain't there no more. Nice car too. *Vooooom* sound it used to make. Momma says there ought to be a noise law against voom cars. I'm glad there isn't. Cars should go voom!"

"What do you mean it ain't there no more?"

"It disappeared. Where to I don't know. Maybe come back in two weeks. It might come back never. Silver car comes once and a while now, but it's ugly and doesn't go voom," said the child, sounding disappointed.

Gus searched through his pockets. He pulled out a sticker. He pealed it off its backing and held it out through the crack on the door. The child snatched it up and placed it on his shirt.

"That was some good investigating you did. Congratulations! You are now an official junior deputy on Sheriff Gus's force. Don't forget: when your momma comes home, tell her to vote for Sheriff Gus."

The child pulled up the section of the shirt with the sticker on it closer to his eyes. "Oh boy!" the child screamed with excitement, and he went running back into the house proper, leaving the door open a crack.

Sheriff Gus closed the front door. He left the porch of number 53 behind and faced the house across the street. A description of the blue Mercedes had been in the newspapers. The state police had talked about it on the nightly news, but still no one in the development called in to report having seen it. Everyone in a nice place like this assumes crimes happened somewhere else. Because of that, the development was a nice place for a murderer to live or have lived.

His friends in the silver car had come and visited the house, but there wasn't a silver car there now. Who were they? Up until a minute ago they were dirty thieving reporters in Gus's mind, but now it seemed they were possibly something worse.

He pulled his riot stick from the back of the truck. Now properly equipped for his task, Gus walked across the street and headed up number 54's driveway. He stopped directly in front of the garage door. The house had a nice, big, double-sized garage door with eight little windows lining the top. The garage was large enough to fit two full-sized cars.

Gus glanced around the neighborhood. There didn't appear to be anyone paying attention to old Gus in the driveway of number 54. He stood up on his tiptoes and looked in through the windows. There were no electric lights on in the garage, but the daylight from outside crept in enough to see inside. There wasn't another body—he hadn't expected there would be—but there was a rather large car-shaped object sitting in the center of the garage. A white sheet was draped over it, totally obscuring the car from view. Outside the garage that sheet might have been to protect the car from the elements. Covering the car inside meant either a dust freak was planning to be gone for a while, or, more likely, someone didn't want a curious passing stranger to know what kind of car was in this garage. Many innocent explanations came to Gus's mind, but none of them did much to convince him they were true.

Gus casually bent over and tried the garage door, but it was locked tight. His lower back sent out a little tingling of pain as he stood back up. Except for his own back, it was all starting to look very promising to Gus.

Gus now turned and casually strolled up to the front porch of the house. He paused again to look around the neighborhood. Not a soul was around. It was the middle of the day, so the majority of kids would still be at school, and their parents would be at work. Gus knew from experience this was a good time of day to do something without drawing a crowd. When he had to evict someone without the neighbors knowing, he chose this time of day.

Gus rang the doorbell to the house. The doorbell was loud and annoying but, more importantly, clearly audible to someone standing on the outside hoping to get in. Nothing happened. Gus listened, and no sounds of movement inside could be heard. He put his ear to the door. There was no television playing. There was no music or radio playing. He couldn't hear a shower running. Gus rang the doorbell again. He waited a full minute in front of the door, expecting nothing to happen. It did.

Gus wandered to the front windows by the door. They were heavily curtained to prevent Gus from looking in. The occupant of the house was a very private type of person. It wasn't unnatural to have a covered car in a locked garage, to not answer a door if you weren't home, or to have curtains. Still, he had it on good authority this was the place he was looking for. Well, if a four-year-old kid could be considered an authority.

Gus wandered off the porch with the same casual stroll and crossed the driveway, heading toward a small rock path that led around the side of the house. He tried the handle on the side door to the garage, but, as expected, it was locked too.

The course of action was clear; Gus should go and try to get a warrant to search the house. He might not be issued a warrant. In the old days things like that didn't matter, but there was an election to be won. The electorate was watching him. You just couldn't break into a person's home during an election. You probably weren't allowed to do it ever. His good cop instincts had led him to this door, but his good cop instincts were telling him to not go in it just yet.

Just then Gus heard a horrible, horrible, blood-curdling scream from inside. The sound was loud, and someone was clearly begging for help. Probably it was just some idiot playing the television too loud, but he had to make sure. The exigent circumstance didn't exactly exist anywhere but in Gus's mind and the official report he was eventually going to write explaining why he broke into the garage. He knew no one in this county would buy that report, and he wouldn't buy it either, but he was also fairly certain this homeowner wasn't about to show up in court and complain the sheriff searched his house without a warrant.

121

Gus smacked the window of the door with his riot stick. The stick bounced off without doing a lick of damage. The glass was tougher than Gus expected. He took a bigger windup and this time shattered the glass, blowing it into the garage. He reached through the window and popped the door lock. He looked around, but the neighborhood was still silent. Gus opened the door and went into the garage.

He walked over to the covered car. He grabbed the white sheet in both hands and yanked it off. He left the sheet in a heap behind the car. The car was a Mercedes, and a dark-colored one at that. Gus flipped a switch near a staircase leading into the house. The car was clearly blue, appeared to have been well kept up, and was , at one time before it was abandoned under a sheet, nicely detailed. This was clearly a car someone had cared about. The license plates were both missing. He walked around to read off the vehicle identification number, but it was missing too. Someone was good at making himself unknown.

Gus would impound the car; somewhere was an identification mark that would tell Gus whose car this was. You couldn't be that careful to remove all the marks off a car and still have a car. Gus was careful not to touch the outside of the car just in case of fingerprints. Though he knew these people wouldn't have left any prints unless it was for a good reason.

He got up close to the driver's-side window. The keys were in the car. The doors were unlocked. Someone was careful, but at the same time not very careful. Clearly they weren't too worried about the car being stolen. He wanted badly to get the keys and pop the trunk, but he'd wait for the forensic team. He didn't want the state police accusing Gus of messing up their evidence. (They would complain anyways, because Gus had gotten here first.)

Gus turned his attention from the car and headed up the staircase into the house. This inside door was unlocked. Breaking and entering was paying off. Gus opened the door to a small hallway that connected the kitchen to the garage. A small doorway marked Pantry was to his right. It was locked from the outside; these people were apparently paranoid about who was eating their groceries.

Gus walked past the pantry into the spacious and modern kitchen. It had a communication island or bar connecting the kitchen to a huge living room. This created the effect of having a great room, which might have been a nice area to entertain guests. Possibly it had entertained three female guests from out of town. Both the kitchen and living room were decorated with expensive modern furniture.

Gus walked over to the giant flat-screen television in the living room. He glanced over the coffee table in front of the television. No magazines that might reveal a name of the house's owner. Gus frowned and turned on the television set. Then he turned it right off. He had ruined the fingerprints that he was pretty sure weren't on it anyways, but he had also put a little collaborative evidence in the room in case he needed it later. He had come in to investigate a sound, after all, and turned the TV off when he discovered it was the source.

He peeked through the curtains in the living room and saw the porch he was standing on moments earlier. He walked over to the front door, which was next to another, smaller door. He went to the kitchen, pulled a napkin from a rack on top of the middle island, headed back to the door, and opened it by using the napkin. The door was hiding nothing. It was a cloak room with nothing inside it. Someone left this place and took their clothes with them. Gus closed the closet door and headed into the rest of the house.

Gus went down a small hallway that led into a series of rooms. Gus opened the door to the first room, a bedroom. The king-size bed was unmade. Three overnight bags lay on the side of the bed, lined up next to each other. The bags were open and had female paraphernalia inside. Gus used the napkin to slide the closet doors open in the bedroom. A few pieces of female clothing hung in the closet. Nothing else, though.

He wandered over to the dresser. It was tall and made of dark wood. The top was cleaned off except for two items: a silver spoon with scorch marks on the bottom, and a polished silver butane lighter. Gus picked it up with the napkin and had a good look at it. It had no identifying marks. Once again someone was trying hard to stress that there was a drug angle in this case. Neither of his town's chief drug lords were exactly agreeing with this fact, though. The spoon, if it was real evidence, did at least narrow down what drugs they bought off Tannehill.

He opened the top drawer to the dresser. It was empty. The whole dresser probably was, thought Gus. He sniffed the top drawer. A faint sent of cologne was still present in the top drawer. It was a man's dresser and clearly a man's drawer. There was no men's clothing left in the room, however. Clearly the man had departed, leaving three overnight bags of women's clothing. Three girls were in this man's room. Lucky for him, thought Gus.

The next room was another bedroom, with a queen-size bed and a long dresser. The room had its own television set and other fancy electronic devices. Gus was heading over to the closet when he noticed a wooden chair in the corner of the room. It looked like one of the kitchen chairs. This was a well-furnished place, and each room so far had a sense of highly exact interior décor. This chair was totally wrong for the room.

Gus walked over to the chair. There were cut ropes hanging from it. At the foot of the chair was a hammer. The hammer's head was crusted with red. There was a lot of dried blood on the floor and the armrests of the chair.

There wasn't any real evidence in the house except this crime scene. Everything else was spotless and empty. Why clean out the closet and then leave this telltale murder scene untouched? Who was this person? He'd call in Dr. Armstrong and the whole criminal investigation team. He'd get the state boys in here as well. It was going to be one big party, and with some luck maybe someone would find a clue to help figure out who did this. You can't get a house, a car, and the rest without someone knowing who you were. It stood to reason this house would lead Gus to that someone.

First, though, Gus wanted to finish having a good look while he was alone with the evidence. He moved over to the next room. It was a den or recreational room. There was a lot of liquor in a minibar. There were half-smoked blunts with lipstick on them in the ashtray. The room smelled like cannabis. Gus looked closely and noticed no blunts without lipstick. No indication a man was here. They were good, whoever they were, at leaving only the clues they wanted to leave; clues that would lead nowhere.

Against one wall was a computer hutch. The computer was gone. Gus leaned down to the ground. There were indentations next to the hutch. Something big and heavy was rolled there. The marks were still on the carpet. Something computer related. Computing was beyond Gus, so it could have been anything. In the wall, though, was a rather fancy plug. Someone had some type of computer connection that wasn't typical, Perhaps it was where the YouTube plugged in. This room had the feel of being the main room of the house. The occupant spent a lot of time here; a lot of time, apparently, doing some serious computing.

Maybe he taped the girls doing god knows what in the bedroom and then made money selling it on the Internet. These three girls, being the type of girl they were, got mad when they found out what he did, and something bad happened in the fight. The guy panicked and someone died. Maybe they all died. The room made sense with the story. But where did the man go? Without a car, taking all his important stuff, and leaving Gus nothing. The house was too clean a murder of panic, and yet the torture room also didn't fit with his little story. Did they make snuff films? Would a girl meet a famous maker of snuff films and intentionally go off with him to be killed? No, thought Gus. The story wasn't coming together.

Gus moved on to the bathroom. It was typical of the house, nice and modern. The house apparently only had this one bathroom, which wasn't typical. The poor owner would have a hard time moving it on the market with only one bathroom. Even harder time after the murder scene made the front page. Then again there were a lot of sick people in the world, so a grisly murder might add appeal to the asking price. Either way Gus had a feeling the owner wouldn't continue to make his payments on this place.

There were three toothbrushes lined up on the sink. There was makeup remover and face cream as well. The bathroom had a feminine feel. There was no trace of anything masculine. In that regard the room fit in with the rest of the house.

Well, time to call in to the office and start the warrant ball rolling, thought Gus. He headed through the kitchen toward the open side door in the garage. There was at least enough evidence here to tie this place with the second murdered girl. He stopped by the fridge. He looked inside at the expiration dates on the food. The milk was new. So were a lot of the items. There was no expired food. That was odd for a refrigerator owned by a murderer who left town not long after the crime. Who would be using the refrigerator of a murderer's house? The people in the silver car, thought Gus. But why?

Gus closed the refrigerator and looked down the short hall that led to the garage. There was still that door marked Pantry. Gus stood in front of it and looked around for a peg with a key on it. There was a peg but no key. Someone had planned to come back with that key to open that door.

Contractors didn't use expensive, solid-built doors inside these quick-build houses. A good, solid hit should break it open. Gus had broken down tougher doors than this one. Gus got up a good head of steam and thrust into the door with his shoulder. The door flung open, leaving Gus unbalanced against it, which led to gravity forcing Gus downward in a heap, face first on the floor.

Gus found himself at the feet of a young woman with a surprised look on her face. She was sitting on the pantry floor. Her hands and feet were tied with rope and she had a gag in her mouth. For once something in the case made sense: you bought fresh food if you were keeping a kidnapped victim alive in your pantry. This young woman was alive, the first actual break of good luck Gus had in a long while. It was probably good luck on her part too, had Gus spent the time to think about things from her perspective. Gus took off the woman's gag.

In a raspy voice, the young woman said, "Water."

"County sheriff. Don't worry, I'll get you out of this closet and get you some water. Just stay calm," said Gus, now not calm and wondering how the TV set story was going to work knowing now that he had zero time to get a real warrant.

Gus picked her up, carried her into the kitchen, and sat her down on top of the island. He found a steak knife and started to cut her free. "Stop moving so much, I ain't an expert in this type of stuff. Now when I free you, remember to stay calm and don't go running off on Sheriff Gus. I'm not the runner I used to be."

Gus got the ropes off her and the young woman remained seated on the island. She was rather oddly calm. Gus went over to the cupboards and got out a glass. He filled it with water from the tap. "I've seen much more dehydrated souls walk out of the high desert than you. You're not that bad off. He must have been feeding you off and on for a while now?"

The young woman took the glass and drank a few sips from it. "Oh, they were good to us, all things considered. They came every day to take care of us. Usually it was both of them together, but occasionally just one of them came. Then two days ago they took Pam with them and just left me in the closet with some supplies. Until then I was calm, but after that, well, I was really worried."

"So someone Cherry met at a party kidnapped you and your three friends after he took you down here from the college?" asked Gus, being careful not to mention to her that her other two friends were dead. It appeared she might not know this fact and might be a lot less calm after hearing the news.

"Oh, no! He didn't do any sort of thing like that. I was talking about his friends. You see, Pam and I were in the game room drinking and having fun. Cherry and Jacob went into his bedroom to...well, you know. Or at least we thought so. I mean, Cherry liked him a lot. She was into him and he was rather nice bringing us down here to have a private party. You can tell a thing like that, can't you?"

Gus nodded his head without trying to interrupt the flow of conversation.

The young woman continued with her story. "Well, we were just having so much fun, you know, like, and his bodyguard came in. She said, like, we looked thirsty and she'd make us some drinks. Dude, she was really friendly like. So we had the drinks and I just can't remember anything else. Total blackout! How embarrassing is that? I guess I partied too much, because the next morning the two of us were on the floor of the game room, and Cherry, the bodyguard, and Jacob were gone. I mean *gone*, as in the whole house had no trace of them and the car was sitting in the garage under a cover. It was true slasher-film weird, if you know what I mean. Pam and I were, like, sort of mad, because, like, we had no way to get back to school.

I didn't want to call my parents, because they would sort of freak. You know what I mean? Someone took our phones and, like, without them I didn't have anyone's number. Those things remember all that stuff for you, so when they're lost, you're lost, if you know what I mean."

"What was the bodyguard's name?" asked Gus.

"I don't know. She might have said it but I don't remember. She was… well, you know, just a personal bodyguard. Like, you don't remember the names of people like that, now do you?"

"Can you describe her at least?"

"Well, she was black and she was fun. She was really nice to us, but she didn't spend a lot of time with us. Stayed in her own room, except when she came in to make the drinks, that is."

"She's the one that drove a black car, right? The black car that is not around anymore?"

"I don't know what kind of car it was. Nothing fancy, but it was black. Jacob's car is in the garage. We, like, thought about taking it back to school, but I didn't want him to think we stole it. Do you want to hear something really gossipy, Mr. Sheriff? Well, Cherry told us Jacob's name isn't really Jacob and his real name is like a secret. Only she guessed at the secret. Pam said it was only lies because everyone needs that aura of importance at a River District party. I don't know what his aura color was but my aura is indigo. Party gossip is pretty interesting stuff, and you know who else was interested? Well, while we were talking about what to do, wouldn't you know it but some of Jacob's friends showed up. They were very interested in everything Jacob related, as it turns out."

"Are these the friends that forced themselves into the house and tied you up?"

"They didn't force their way in at all, we let them in. They were his friends, after all, so we didn't see, like, any harm letting them in. They gave the place a good look over, and we explained to them our own problem about getting back to college, and they said like they would help us out after taking care of a few things. Let me tell you, that was, like, the perfect answer to our problem. It all seemed really nice and friendly, so we thought, like, nothing of it."

"So what happened when these friends of Jacob came back that ended with you in the closet?" said Gus, trying to keep her talking while she was calm and chatty.

"Yeah, there were, like I said, two of them. They had the same stupid accent as Jacob did. European-like, but they talked English, not like Spanish or something foreign. Well, later that night they came back and, well, they acted different, dude. They asked a lot more questions about Jacob that we didn't know. I mean, we, like, barely knew the guy, and that's what we kept telling them. You'd think, like, being his friends, they'd know the answers better than us, like, you know? They kept going on and on and getting madder and madder—where was he, where was his computer, who were the two of us, how many people were watching over him, who was he working for...a lot of questions. They just wouldn't believe our answers, and I spoke the God-honest truth to them too, because, like, we were supposed to be friends, or at least friends of friends. Well, they got furious now, and hitching a drive back to school from them was looking doubtful, so we tried to leave to find a bus station or something. But they wouldn't let us leave. Before we knew it we ended up tied up in the pantry. They only let us out a few times every day to eat a little and go to the bathroom. Then two days ago they took Pam away and told me Jacob had it coming to him. I never saw Pam again after that. What do Jacob having it coming and Pam disappearing have to do with each other? I'll admit, until seeing you I had been really worried. Jacob's friends are just a bunch of assholes."

Gus thought that seemed to be an understatement.

She gave him as honest and straightforward a description as to what was going on as she probably could. It was time to get her out of here, and by the time he got to talk to her again, if he did get to talk to her again, her story would be clouded by knowing her friends were dead, learning that Jacob was a true asshole too, and being asked tons of questions by a handful of different authorities. If there was more story to get, it was unlikely anyone would get it as unfiltered as the information Gus just received.

Gus had always figured Michelle, Pam, and Cherry were just unfortunate victims in this whole affair, and for once he was proven right. Whatever was going on was beyond the three of them.

"OK, it's time for us to get out of here."

As Gus finished that sentence, the front door knob made a noise like someone unlocking it from outside on the porch.

"Michelle, I want you to get behind this kitchen island and keep your head down until I give you a sign. Then I want you to run like a bat out of hell past the pantry and into the garage. Trust old Sherriff Gus; you understand that?"

She nodded her head and quickly did as she was told. "What's, like, going to happen?"

Gus pulled out his gun. He pointed at the front door. If he was lucky, they hadn't noticed the broken window of the side door. If he was really lucky, they'd walk right into him hands down and unarmed.

There were continued noises on the porch. They were taking a long time getting in the front door. Gus was relieved—maybe it wasn't the "friends" of Jacob. Then the front door lock popped and the handle started to turn. The door opened and revealed a human figure holding a gun. Gus didn't wait to get acquainted better; he shot his gun at the figure in the doorway. He unloaded four bullets and the figure fell backward out of view. Michelle took it as the sign to move and ran down the hall into the garage. Gus quickly moved behind her as the front window glass exploded with bullets. Someone was blindly unloading an automatic weapon into the living room.

Gus closed the door to the house as he passed through it. He was winded but he didn't have time to think about it. The two of them now found themselves in the garage. Gus thought better than to run out the side door. If luck was on his side, the gunmen would run after them through the open front door. Gus quickly came up with a plan B.

"Michelle, please get into the back seat of the car."

Gus followed her inside. The doors were open and the keys were still in it. He went on speaking to Michelle without looking at her.

"Just lie down across that back seat and try not to look up. There is going to be more shooting."

Gus started the car and floored the gas pedal with the car in neutral. That should gain the attention of Jacob's friends, he thought. The wheels squealed across the garage floor, but Gus held the car back. He waited. Black smoke from the tires was filling the room. Gus started to worry that the tires would blow before the shooter arrived. Finally bullets started ripping through the door leading from the house. With proof that the bad guys were inside the house, Gus popped the car into gear and accelerated through the garage door. The front windshield shattered in place, turning into a series of cobwebs. A few small pieces broke off and flew into Gus's face. As Gus reached the bottom of the driveway he spun the car with a hard turn to the left and slammed on the brakes. The car skidded to a stop. Between the Mercedes and the house, a silver sedan was parked on the side of the road. It nicely blocked the blue Mercedes from a good line of sight from the house. Gus put the Mercedes into park and hurried as fast as his body could move out of the car to brace himself behind the silver car. He had his gun out again and waited patiently for his friend to appear. Soon a figure appeared in the front doorway. The figure didn't have a gun at the ready, as he was probably expecting Gus to have kept right on driving. Really, a sensible man would have done that. Lesson one of how to handle a dangerous situation was to get away from the danger as soon as possible. However, Gus wasn't driving at full speed down the street in a rather fast limited-edition blue Mercedes.

The figure realized this fact too late, and Gus fired a shot dead into the figure's chest. The figure stumbled over the body already on the porch. Gus fired one more time. The figure tumbled down the stairs and crumbled into a heap at the bottom of the stairs. There had been just two figures at Mike's gas station that day in a silver car, and now Gus had just shot two people dead. Hopefully that was all of them.

Gus put his gun away and for the first time he noticed the wave of exhaustion strike his body. He looked over at the Mercedes to see Michelle's head pop up from the back seat. Gus's heart was pounding. He slumped down the side of the silver vehicle. The kidnappers and possible murderers were now very dead.

Then he heard a funny kind of screaming. He looked up. Across the street was a four-year-old kid dancing on the lawn going, "Vroom, vroom, bang, bang! Do it again, do it again!"

Gus left Michelle in the driveway of number 53. He needed to get his look at the suspects before the zoo arrived. The first victim was at the bottom of the steps. Gus hit him in the head with that last shot, and it made for a rather bloody mess. Gus did a quick pat-down. There didn't feel to be anything interesting in the guy's pockets. Gus went up to the porch and looked over the second person. He was hit three times in the body. He had left the keys in the door, where they were still hanging. Gus bent over to pat the body down. His lower back went again with a shooting pain. He was rewarded for his trouble, however. Under the victim's suit coat was a manila folder with a hole in it. It was slightly stained with blood. It looked like Gus's manila folder. It was evidence, but it was Gus's evidence, and for the moment he wanted it back.

A shot rang out over the sheriff's head and hit the porch post. The shot startled the sheriff, and out dropped the manila folder from his hands.

A thin reedy voice shouted out from behind Gus, "Stay right where you are or I'll plug you good! Put up those hands where I can see them, you hooligan. Now turn around really slow. I'm Frank Brady, chief officer of the neighborhood watch, and I'm making a citizen's arrest!"

Gus did as he was told and turned around to see a fat, short, balding man pointing an expensive semiautomatic pistol right at Gus. The blood started to trickle down Gus's face again.

"Look, idiot, I'm the sheriff. You neighborhood watchers know what a law-enforcement officer is, don't you?"

"Well, how am I supposed to know you're the sheriff?" Frank was the type to talk with his hands, so the gun wavered while he spoke.

"I don't know, maybe this badge here on my chest. Maybe the outfit I'm standing here wearing. Maybe that vehicle parked over there across the street. I thought the word 'watch' was in your job description. How good a watch person can you be if you the miss the totally obvious clues? Two hardened murderers have been living in this house the better part of a week, and you watch people manage to assault the sheriff when he comes to investigate them. Son, your 'watch' is about as useful to law enforcement as an abstinence-only pamphlet is in a whorehouse." Gus stopped speaking and put his one hand down as far as to put the rag back over his bleeding head.

Frank put his gun back in his open-carry holster. "I'm sorry about that, Sheriff. Now that I got a good look at you of course I recognize you. I saw you in person at that debate last night. You're the surly fellow that knows how to give people the what for. That's what this county needs, if you ask me. Dressing nice and looking pretty for the audience isn't going to solve this county's problem? Hell no, it isn't! There are too many minorities robbing honest taxpayers and using the general welfare to buy drugs and murdering our citizens. That's why we need a straight shooter that will put those fucking punks in their place."

"The place I have to put these two *Caucasian* suspects at the moment is the county morgue, so if you don't mind, I'll start doing that. Why don't you run along back down to the road and costume playact with your other little watch friends? If you're really good to me, I'll let you act like some sort of crowd control."

Gus shooed the bigoted bald man that had just committed attempted assault with a deadly weapon away from the crime scene. Stupid people were always ignoring the rule of law and taking justice matters into their own hand, thought Gus. He bent over and picked up the manila folder again. The folder's information was compromised with a bullet hole, and the crime scene was compromised by an idiot with a gun. He was going to need a whole lot of yellow tape.

CHAPTER 6

Gus was again spending a morning lying on the sofa in pain. He assured himself that the majority of the pain was due to the sofa and not that he was an old man that just the day before foolishly played the action hero. It was occurring to Gus that it was a good thing he was going to lose the election and end his over-the-hill action and adventure days. He had four Band-Aids on the cut to his head, from the splintering windshield, and three more on minor cuts to his arms. He was feeling sort of happy this morning. As far as he could tell from the news people on his TV set, the state police had declared that the murders in his county were solved. But the story didn't exactly match with the information Gus received from Michelle yesterday.

The official report was extremely streamlined; all the dots connected to the two dead men. But how could it be over when the owner of the blue car was somewhere out there? They said the blue car belonged to one of the two dead men. This wasn't exactly what Michelle told him yesterday. Gus had spent the night bleeding and typing out the facts, but they didn't apparently matter to anyone else.

The way Gus figured it, the two people he killed in the development were looking for that other man. They kidnapped those two young women and apparently tortured one to death trying to find out where he was. They tailed Gus around, thinking he knew where the guy was. The question remaining to Gus was, where was he? Gus still had no information to solve

135

that. He wouldn't get any help in the matter, because now the matter was officially solved.

Also, who killed the first victim? The official report glossed over that and said it was one of the two dead men. This was fantastical to Gus. It was much more likely the unknown man and/or possibly his bodyguard were at fault.

The state police were not releasing the information on the two dead men to the public. This was mostly because, as Gus saw it, there was none to release. They were dead. They had no fingerprints on file. Their car was not registered to anyone. The DNA testing was still being done. It was amazing how fast officials could obtain lab results when they really wanted to obtain them. Perhaps it was fantastical fast, but the official report on the two men was mostly closed, barring something on the genetic evidence. They were, according to the official report, a couple of unknown mystery men. So far no one had claimed them as their own, and who was likely to claim two dead murderers? It was something found in a badly written spy novel. To Gus they were likely exactly what they appeared to be: a couple of paid thugs.

Who was paying them was a complete mystery, and if that mystery were ever solved it wouldn't be shared with Gus anyways. Whoever he was, he was the kind of guy other people wanted dead, and people were willing to kill to make sure he got dead faster. At this point Gus wasn't far from wanting the mystery man dead too. If everyone involved was lucky, the thugs had got to him and the matter was done and really finished. But Gus wanted to know that it was.

Gus's rest and contemplation on the sofa were interrupted by the dreaded phone.

"Sheriff Gus here."

"Gus, it's Marty. What have you got for me?"

"You read your own paper, don't you?"

"We put the state police report in the paper today, but I don't believe it. I never believe anything official, because the best stories are all off the record. What do you say, Gus, is there more to this?"

"Well, there were one or two things that don't appear to tie up with what you wrote and what I know, but maybe it is just as well that the whole thing is over. Don't you think it not being sex maniacs but hired murderers out for who knows what is better for the general mental psyche of the county?"

"But why kill those girls, and in such different ways? Were they high on drugs? Working for the drug gangs? Some sort of sadomasochists out for fun? There is so much information we don't know that could be used to sell a story! So what do you say?"

"Maybe if they find out who they are, they'll tell us. As for me, I'm trying to figure out what I'll be doing when this sheriff thing is all over."

"Now, Gus, don't be like that. The debate was pure genius, and now certain parts of the county are actually pulling for you. Saving that girl might actually put you over the top."

"Well, I'd like to thank you for helping me with the nasty thing you put on your editorial page."

"It's just business. Speaking of business, I got to find some other business if this business is all done. Might have to start back on full election coverage. You have a quote from our new county hero?"

"I'm too tired to think of one. Just think of something appropriate for me to have said."

"Will do, Gus, will do." And with that Marty hung up.

Gus lay back on the sofa, ready to get more rest, when the doorbell rang. He made a sluggish walk to his front door and peeked out the window to see Deputy Drew on the porch. Gus reluctantly opened the door.

"Hi, Sheriff! Lupita said you were a lazy slob and wouldn't be coming into the office today and I was to deliver these papers to you."

Gus grabbed a folder from Deputy Drew. "What are they?"

"Got me, Sheriff, I didn't read them. I try to get as little involvement with reading as possible."

"That sounds good to me. Let me help you out on accomplishing your goal." Gus slammed the door in his face.

Gus lay down on the sofa and leafed through the folder. It was the latest official report, a boring read. Much of Gus's input was ignored. Marty had been generous, as the report could lead one to believe that Gus's actions might have endangered the kidnapping victim, that he might have broken and entered, and that he might have used unlawful deadly force. It didn't directly say it, but a paper or a DA could have picked that storyline out if they so chose.

Gus was growing weary reading it and his eyes were having trouble remaining open, until he hit the last page. It wasn't part of the official report; it was a note from Deputy Costner: "Here's that information on the plate you had me run a few days back." Gus rubbed his eyes to try to wake up a little. Gus was so busy on his idea about needles and haystacks he forgot all about the license-plate check. Gus read through the note. It was pretty much just what Tannehill had told him: the plates belonged to a corporate car, a gray van from the McGruffin Corporation. The deputy had even scribbled a phone number at the bottom of the sheet and the address. The company was out of state, just as Gus had been told. The election and the murderer were related, as they both had the same out-of-state financial backer. Gus bet Marty would have loved to know that.

Gus picked up his cell phone and rang the number. The phone rang and rang but no one answered. It was close to noon now. Gus decided he'd drive out to Constantine's café and then take the highway out of state. The McGruffin Corporation deserved an official visit from the sheriff's office.

Gus called into the office and left Deputy Costner in charge for a few days. He headed north out of state to find out who the McGruffin Corporation was and why they didn't like him or young women. The long period in his car seat was not helping Gus's back pain. But Gus was too lost in thought to notice his back. Why some corporation from so far away cared about who was sheriff in a small county was a mystery. A mystery made more mysterious now that it also had something to do with the hired guns and the man with the blue car. It was a mystery Gus could actually do something about, as the question of Lance Daniels and his campaign finances wasn't a case officially closed by the state. Even if it were, the case only really closed when Gus closed it.

Gus pulled off the highway into an unfamiliar residential district. He was lost and confused, so he pulled off the road to consult his road maps. The county had offered Gus a free installation of a GPS device for his sheriff truck, but he had figured if he wanted something that continuously gave him advice while he was driving he would remarry. A pile of maps lay unfolded across the passenger seat of the truck. Gus pulled out the one he thought was the correct map for the area. He had circled McGruffin headquarters correctly on the map while eating at the Constantine café the day before. Judging from his map-reading skill, he wasn't that badly off course; the headquarters was just a few blocks away. Seemed odd to Gus to stick your company headquarters in a residential district, but maybe this state had zoning laws that allowed corporations to put their headquarters in stupid places.

Gus put the truck into gear to start moving again when sirens came on behind his vehicle. In the rearview mirror he saw a police car pulling up behind him. Gus turned the truck engine off and watched a clean, polished officer step out of his squad car. The police officer paused to read the sheriff logo on the side of the truck. He then appeared to write down Gus's license plate number. Finally he moved up to Gus's window.

"Can I have your license and registration, sir?"

"Is there a problem, officer?" Gus leaned his wallet out the window showing his sheriff badge.

The officer took the badge and read it over. "I've never heard of that county before. You aren't from around these parts, are you?"

"Well, I'm from way down south. I was here looking for McGruffin Corporation. You wouldn't happen to know where that is?" asked Gus.

The officer handed back Gus's badge. "I'm sorry, but you are illegally parking here. You're going to have to move this or I'll have to write you a ticket."

Gus frowned and started the truck up.

"Hey, wait up a minute," said the officer. "I'm going to still have to see your license and registration. I have to make sure you are who you say you are."

Gus turned the truck back off. Gus handed him back the wallet. "They are both in there somewhere."

"You'll have to take them out for me."

Gus took back the wallet and searched around for his license and registration. After some moments he found them both and handed them back to the officer. The officer returned to his squad car. Gus was not in a very good mood, since this had little to do with parking and a lot to do with pointless law-enforcement games they did to each other to make sure each knew their place. Gus was in this officer's territory. The officer had profiled him as the type that might make trouble. Trouble was a completely relative term. The area likely had someone around here up to no good if viewed from the perspective of an outsider. This officer was just making sure Gus didn't make trouble for that someone because they had a local understanding. Gus was helpless outside of his county to do much but sit around while the little computer ratted out all of Gus's personal information to the officer. It didn't matter how fast the computer ratted on Gus, because the officer was going to take his sweet time getting back to Gus. The longer Gus waited in purgatory for the final judgment the longer his imagination would torture him. A ticket was alright, but Gus couldn't afford to spend a night in jail. When it came to bullies and the bullied it was generally more fun to be the bully. Finally the officer got back out of the squad car and made the walk back to Gus's driver window.

"OK, everything checks out. Now I'm going to let you off with a warning this time."

Gus smiled. "I am truly sorry, officer." He took his information back from the officer and threw it on the passenger seat. He started up the truck again.

"Now hold on, didn't be in such a rush to leave me. We aren't done just yet. I need to ask you a few routine questions since you are an out of state driver."

Gus understood he didn't need to be doing anything. The officer wanted to do it and he was enjoying it. Gus knew the feeling from the officer's point of view all to well. He turned off the ignition once again. Gus continued his smile, "I'll gladly answer any question you have."

"Have you transported any exotic fruits or vegetables into this state?"

"I'm not really that big an eater of fruits or vegetables. I rarely transport them from the grocery store to my house yet alone transporting them across state lines. I think you can sleep easy knowing your state is safe from an illegal fruiting."

"I wish I could take your word for it but I'm going to have to take a look inside your vehicle. Could you please step out of the vehicle?"

Gus knew he could get out of his vehicle. He also knew there were no rogue carrots riding along with him for the officer to find. The real question was would he? The game had reached a critical step where jail almost certainly awaited Gus if he got out of the vehicle. This officer was going to keep pushing him until he responded.

"I don't think you need to look in this truck. You didn't want me illegally parking at this curb and the stupid thing about all this is, had you not bothered me I would not have spent the past thirty minutes doing just that. So if you want to end the current violation of law in your little patch of land then I suggest you let me drive away from here."

The officer's face was stern. He leaned into the driver side window, "How about you get out of your vehicle and go sit in the back of my car instead?"

"First you will drive me down to your station. Next I'll get photographed and fingerprinted. After all the photographic evidence has been taken you're then free to rough me up at your leisure. Then you'll stick me in the drunk tank with some of the local color to spend the night. In the morning you won't press any charges and I'll be free to go, but I won't be able to go anywhere because you will have towed my vehicle. So I'll have to go to the impound lot and buy my truck out of jail. Thank you, Officer, what an important moral lesson I've just learned. Now that I've learned it, can I leave?"

The officer didn't respond right away. He watched Gus behind his mirrored sunglasses.

"You should really learn to respect the laws, as we are all supposed to be role models for the general citizenry, and I don't stand for anyone coming here breaking the peace in my neighborhood. You do understand my meaning? Now move this piece of junk off of my curb!"

Gus had gambled and it worked. Gus knew from experience it didn't always work. Did any of these games save lives? They didn't appear to. Gus would have to remember to remind himself of that next time he found his role reversed.

He drove through a rather nice old-style suburban neighborhood. Finally he found the number he was looking for, but the number belonged to another rather nice-looking wood-paneled house. On the lawn was a sign that read Corporate Headquarters. Whatever this company was, it appeared they were spending more on Lance Daniels than they were on their own corporate image. Gus pulled the sheriff truck into the driveway. He could have tried leaving it curbside but decided he didn't want to risk a second ticket in this neighborhood. As he got out of his truck, the squad car made another appearance driving down the street and passed the house Gus had just parked at. They were a nosy and suspicious type in this neighborhood.

Gus went up to the front door and rang the bell. Nothing happened. Gus didn't want to illegally break into a second house this week, so he rang the bell again and added a few pounds on the door with his fist. At last he could hear movement on the other side of the door. A middle-aged woman in a gray flannel dress and black horn-rimmed glasses opened the door. She scowled at Gus from behind the glasses. This neighborhood really knew how to project warmth to a visitor.

The lady in gray spoke first, with a stern tone. "I am sorry, there was no need to keep ringing and banging on the door; I was moving as fast I could. I wasn't expecting any visitors today. We don't get visitors here. I can't remember the last time anyone visited this place besides me."

Gus flashed the sheriff badge and motioned to come inside. The lady backed away from the front door and Gus took this as an affirmation that it was all right for him to enter the premises.

The inside of the corporate headquarters was a disappointment. The contents of the house appeared at first glance to be nothing but a cluttered mess. The main entrance area was stacked in a maze of three-drawer metallic filing cabinets. On top of each filing cabinet was a small wooden cubby. The cubbies were overflowing with papers. The only open area in the main room was near the door, where the lady had carved out space for a small metal-framed desk. The desk contained a small computer and a telephone.

It occurred to Gus this woman might be one of those hoarders. He had been in a few hoarders' homes in his time as sheriff. Gus didn't understand mentally ill people like that. There didn't seem anything particularly precious about these people's stuff. It seemed to Gus these were people that couldn't find it in their heart to throw anything away, and thus they threw their whole lives away in a mountain of crap instead. Society had taught them to consume, and that is what they did, with no rhyme or reason to what to do with it after it was all acquired.

On closer inspection the cluttered mess appeared different, so if this was a hoarder, it was an odd sort of hoarder. Hoarders usually just had piles of pointless crap stacked floor to ceiling. This hoarder must be a rather anal neat freak. Her hoard was apparently sorted and filed. This was just what Gus wasn't looking for, another mystery.

"Is the whole house like this?" asked Gus.

"Yes. This is the busy season, officer, so if you'd be so kind as to state your business…I am a very busy woman. I have several international faxes arriving in the fax room, and I really need to get them sorted, filed, or shredded."

Gus scratched his head a little and continued looking around the room. "I am looking for the McGruffin Corporation headquarters. They list this address as the corporate address. That isn't some kind of mistake, is it? You are the McGruffin Corporation?"

"Mistake? I can assure you this place is not in the habit of making mistakes. Of course this is the McGruffin Corporation headquarters. I am, however, not the McGruffin Corporation. Not that I am not incorporated. Only a fool these days would go around not incorporated. If you are seeking the McGruffin Corporation, you will find them third row in and second from the end on the left. I believe Wednesday I got a fax for them and filed it in their corporation mailbox."

Gus looked over the sea of filing cabinets in a state of confusion. "Where again is this corporation?"

The woman beamed her eyes at Gus in frustration. "Come along, I will show you."

The woman entered the maze and effortlessly navigated her way directly to a cubby on one of the filing cabinets. She pointed Gus to the stack of little cubbies three rows in and second from the left. Each one had a name on it. Not a person's name but the name of a corporation, or at least something that sounded business-like and official. She was a hoarder, but she horded corporations, as if they were collectable cups from a fast-food place. The whole house was filled with filing cabinets and little bins with company names.

"No offense, lady, but I want to see the real company headquarters. I came here to get some answers from these McGruffin people, and I can't talk to a filing cabinet. I have official sheriff business to ask them, and I don't want to waste any more time being blinded by this illegal front," said Gus in his own stern voice.

The woman was not to be intimidated. She merely crossed her arms over her chest and returned stern voice for stern voice. "Illegal? You are very much mistaken. I assure you in this state this is all perfectly above-board and legal. This corporation is not a front for illegal activity, it is a perfectly legal enterprise that caters to corporations that seek a tax shelter from more tax-unfriendly states. As to the whole building we are stand-ing in, I assure you I'm in total charge here. I do the phone answering, the email answering, the fax answering, and I make sure all of these cor-porations are properly filed in the tax records of this state. There is no other 'they' that is hiding behind the scenes, as this whole enterprise is in perfect legal standing, and as a person in charge of the law I would assume you would know all this already." She had emphasized the last point most of all.

Gus was a little aware of the concept of tax shelters, and whether they were legal or not was a matter of moral authority that Gus didn't have the power to enforce. A front was a front, and it not only hid a company from taxes but apparently from having a public face. Still, there had to be someone behind all the fronts. Legally the papers would have real names on them.

Gus asked the woman, "So these cabinets have all the legal papers in them that make this here business straight and legal. I would like to look over McGruffin Corporation's legal forms to make sure everything is as up and up as you claim."

The woman tugged a little on her gray flannel jacket. "I can assure you they are, and without a search warrant I do not see how you can legally request any official record from any company in here. If that is all, I will show you back to the door, as I have much more filing to do today."

Gus looked over the filing cabinets. They were pretty cheaply constructed. Not that much different than the ones in his office. He remembered when Deputy Drew lost the key to the DUI-files cabinet. They managed to open the cabinet with a few swift kicks, collapsing it in far enough that the lock simply broke from its catch. The other option was shooting the lock, but in all the years he had been in law enforcement he had never opened a lock by shooting it. He was skeptical of the practicality of even being able to really shoot off a lock. Either way, a little kicking incident could hardly get him much time in the local jail.

Gus delivered a hard kick into the face of the filing cabinet. The woman in gray flannel was not amused and started a counterattack of fists to Gus's arm, but her flailing wasn't much to be concerned about. Gus stepped back and saw the face of the cabinet was indeed smashed in pretty affectively. Gus placed three more hard boots to the face of the drawer. If it remained locked or not was all but academic at this point, as Gus had collapsed the front inward and thus created enough space to fish out a piece of paper from the cabinet. The woman stopped her useless assault and started verbally threatening Gus instead.

Gus looked over the paper he had fished out. It wasn't much of a letter. Indeed it was nothing but gibberish. The entire message was random letters, symbols, and numbers that filled the whole page. It could be in a code of some sort, thought Gus. Gus turned to the woman. "Are all the correspondences like this one?"

The woman was no longer simply stern. She was incensed, with a bitter hatred for the man busting up her perfectly running fake machine. "How dare you look at private correspondence between these private corporations and me? What we do is perfectly legal, and what you are doing is perfectly illegal! I shall answer no questions from a brute like you! Instead I shall call the local police and have you arrested!"

Gus looked once more at the gibberish letter. There was one item on the page that was actually crystal clear and not in code/random gibberish. The name on the bottom read "Sigmund Smudge; President, McGruffin Corporation."

Gus crumbled the piece of paper up into a ball. "So sorry. I didn't mean to cause trouble for Mr. McGruffin and you. Here's your correspondence back. I don't think it's very important, but if you can't live without it, here it is." Gus bounced it off the woman's head.

She stood there too furious to move and call the police. She fumed as Gus walked back out the maze and passed through her front door, slamming it on the way out as loudly as he could. Alone once more in the room, she let out an expletive and then, neatly as possible, unfolded the paper and slid it back into its cabinet. She gave a few tugs on the front of the cabinet to try to bend it back in place before giving up on the futile task.

Gus was on his long trip back home and decided he was a safe enough distance from the scene of his latest crime to thinks things over. He parked the truck in the parking lot of a superstore. Out front they sold cheap slices of pizza and sodas. Gus pocketed the receipt so he could be reimbursed for the meal as an office expense. It might be his last official expense account, so he tried to enjoy the cheap pizza. He cracked the driver's-side window to keep it a habitable temperature inside. His other window was a clear plastic bag taped into place, since he hadn't the time to replace it yet after the debate night break-in. One rolled-down window didn't provide much of a breeze, but he wanted to be alone while he ate and thought over what it was he'd learned.

Legal or not, the company was obviously a front for someone or something. Who needs a front company? A criminal was the obvious answer, but of course these days even presidential candidates took advantage of tax shelters in tax-friendly areas. So while it could be a criminal enterprise, it could be something or someone very legal. Was there an obvious criminal in this case? Trash Tannehill possibly was involved. Gustavo's gang might be involved. But then his gang ratted out Trash, and Trash didn't have any dirt to do the same the other way. That made Trash more likely. But why would Trash plant evidence in the coroner's office to implicate himself? Maybe the evidence was real and they all overlooked it that first day in the field. It was a very tiny vial. But Trash wouldn't hire two out-of-town hit-men to try to find a missing person in his own county. He didn't have need to, as he had plenty of thugs that could beat up women and pull triggers.

Gus then had a little idea. Trash wasn't half bad-looking and had the money to dress the part of a famous rich man. He might like hanging out in the swanky parts of the city, as there were vastly nicer looking women there than on his ranch. He could pretend to be whoever he wanted to pick up a girl. The missing man's car was seen by Antonio or one of his spies on Tannehill's ranch. Gus had only Trash's word they were there to buy drugs. He might plant some drugs to make the story true. Trash had a lot of bodyguards; he might even have a black female bodyguard. Also, drug dealers might have thugs out to kill him.

It was a pretty good story; it almost all fit. It was at least better than the official report that closed the case.

But Gus shook his head no. Why would hired killers need to follow Gus and break into Gus's truck and steal his files to find Trash Tannehill? Anyone in the county could find Trash Tannehill. They certainly wouldn't need to torture a girl for information to find out about Trash. It was a nice story, but just a story.

Then again maybe there was one other person he could talk too. Lance Daniels had entered the race long before the girl was found. It would mean this corporation front was already planning a move on the town before the murders for some reason. Why? Was it to have a sheriff in place to protect them from hired killers? Lance Daniels looked like a lot of things, but was he just another store-bought front? Lance Daniels's connection to the fictitious Sigmund Smudge's fantasy corporation was one of many puzzles possibly made from the pieces.

Well, entrepreneurs apparently used tax shelters too. Sigmund Smudge's business would be legal or mostly legal. International companies didn't have to exist anywhere, or could exist everywhere, for that matter. His missing man could be Sigmund Smudge, millionaire. But if that were true, Marty would have known the name. Well, then the name was as fake as the front company. If Jacob was a fake name, then maybe Smudge was too.

Gus could talk to Lance Daniels, but Gus was pretty sure that with the case officially closed, Lance's mouth would be even more closed. Even when he did open it, it was generally to say a lot of nothing anyways. He had no reason to talk to Gus. The longer Lance Daniels said nothing, the sooner Lance Daniels would only have to answer to Sheriff Daniels. Trash, on the other hand, might talk for the sake of talking. And at least he'd give Gus some free beer for the effort.

The three young girls now attracted Gus's attention. They thought this charade of a man was famous, but did they know he was? Gus only had secondhand information from Mandy and Michelle to confirm that Cherry *thought* he was. Once again, Cherry could have been duped, but Gus couldn't be sure she was. Not only Trash but any person could have said anything at one of those parties; lord knows, people probably did. That is what Pam had said. Pam was the one killed by the hitmen. The one they figured was the smarter of the two. Pam wasn't a fool. Who else has two men trying to kill him but a criminal?

Gus now vaguely remembered the two in the car that followed him. They were in the coroner's parking lot just before the drug evidence was found. They might have had the opportunity to plant the evidence. They were obviously following Gus around that first day but not much after. But maybe that's only what Gus thought. They might have been better at tracking after the first day. They could have been moving Gus around town, having him talk to the people they didn't want to be observed talking to. But what did Trash know, or what did they think he knew? A license plate number that didn't lead anywhere. What else could Trash have known that they were hoping Gus would find out? Maybe nothing.

Trash was helpful that day Gus talked to him, but not too helpful. Trash was cagey by nature, being in an illegal business venture, but had he been too cagey. Gus had left feeling there was more to get. The more Gus sat eating his slice, the more it felt likely. Cherry saw through Jacob's fake disguise, so maybe Trash did too. If he did, Trash would keep it close to the vest, because apparently Jacob had at least access to Smudge's money; thus there were bribing opportunities.

There really only seemed like one thing left to do: drive back and talk to Trash. Either he had the missing piece to the puzzle or not. If not, it was likely Gus was at the end, because Sigmund Smudge was not likely to materialize in the flesh.

It was past midnight when Gus arrived back in his county. The sensible thing was to go home and tackle Trash in the morning. He probably was going to say nothing, so why not hear nothing fully rested? But Gus couldn't dodge the feeling Trash knew more, and Gus wanted to know what Trash knew.

He must've recognized the murderer more than he said. If you knew a man that was trying to hide, then you were in an opportunistic spot to make a buck off them. Trash liked making a buck more than he liked making drugs. No, Gus wouldn't let it pass until morning. He'd have it out with Trash right now in the dark.

The compound would be even more heavily guarded at night. Gus had driven by before at night. There were motion-sensor floodlights on the driveway and a few gunmen tucked off in the bushes by the side of the road. Driving in too fast was risky, as some knucklehead could shoot him. Gus would need to come up the drive very cautiously. Still he figured they wouldn't be dumb enough to shoot impulsively at a sheriff's truck if Gus made sure they recognized it as such. The best approach was to make it real obvious to even the dumbest thug by turning his truck's sirens and official lights on.

Gus turned off the highway and onto the interstate toward Trash's ranch. There wasn't another vehicle on the road this far into ranch land at this time of night. It felt an unusually long trip, being alone on the road in the dark, although the drive to the ranch was only twenty minutes.

The sides of the road remained very dark, and eeriness was setting in. It was occurring to Gus that the Tannehill ranch was feeling too dark. Gus made a snap decision to change the plan. Keep the lights off and keep silent, for there was something up tonight in ranch land.

Gus pulled the truck over to the side of the road. He knew he was close to the entrance of the ranch. There should have been floodlights on already out in the fields and up at the main house. Gus turned his headlights off and let his eyes adjust to the blackness of the night. The whole ranch land around him was very black. The moon had not come up yet, and the stars shone brightly in the clear night sky. He sat watching the ranch for some sign of life. It occurred to him that maybe he should have gone straight home and tackled Trash in the morning.

He rolled down his window and listened quietly for anything in the cooling night air. In the distance he could hear faint cries. Gus got excited for only a moment before he realized they weren't human noises. The sound was distant and animal related. They were from a ranch on the other side of the compound. They were probably from Dick Dresden's emu ranch. Gus didn't know what the fuck an emu was. Perhaps tonight was a good night to pay the emus a visit and see what an emu ranch was all about.

Gus started up the truck again. He drove with the headlights off as he passed the Tannehill ranch. Gus was born and raised in this county. He could drive ranch land blindfolded, so even by starlight he felt comfortable driving without headlights. He passed the compound as quietly as his truck would let him. Once he put a half mile between him and Trash's ranch, he flipped his headlights on and increased his velocity. At a fork in the road, Gus took a right and headed to the neighboring ranch.

He could see lights on at Dresden's place from the road. Lights on at the Dresden's ranch and lights off at the Trash's ranch meant something was happening at the Tannehill compound.

It was past midnight now. He pulled up the Dresden driveway and parked the truck behind the barn so no one would see it from the road if they were looking. He got out of the truck and started in the direction of the fence between the two ranches. He stopped and nearly kicked himself. He went back to the truck and opened the back. He found his black sheriff's bag. He pulled out a pair of large industrial wire cutters and grabbed his rifle from its case. It was a nice rifle that he had gotten from his wife as an anniversary present. He had bought her a new washer and drier.

Gus walked through the pasture toward the fence line between the two properties. To Gus emus looked like giant chickens, only not as attractive. He passed through them as quietly as he could. The emus kept their distance from Gus. Some were sleeping, and a few wandered around paying rapt attention to the idiot wandering in the dark through their pasture. Gus thought as animals go, emus were not a good-smelling one. Still, the journey was making him a little hungry for some fried chicken. He reached the fence between the properties.

The farm had an eight-foot-high picket fence. This was either to keep the emus in or to block out the site of Trash's meth lab, as the sight of those tended to bring down property values. On top of the fence was razor wire. Gus tried imagining himself climbing over the fence. The Gus in his imagination was in much better shape to do the climbing. Instead real-life Gus continued down the fence line until he came to the aqueduct that flowed through the two properties; the aqueducts from the river were the lifeline to the ranch land. The picket fence ended at the aqueduct and continued again on the other side of the artificial river bank. Razor wire filled the gap in the fence and was strung across the top of the flowing water.

Gus languidly waded into the water. The water flow was pushing him off balance, and eventually he went totally underwater. He emerged at the fence line. The razor wire ran underwater as well. He began cutting the bottommost fence wire. The water flow was pushing him into the razor wire, and Gus worked fast so as not to be shredded on the emu farm. The tension on the wire caused it to snap when Gus released it with a snip. He cut another, and the third wire nearly took Gus's nose off as it went by. Relieved at the close call, Gus decided to make due with just the bottom three wires missing. He ducked his body under the water and swam between the two properties.

Incredibly short of breath and panting for air, Gus arrived on the other side of the fence. Swimming through the water took too much energy and made too much noise, so Gus moved quickly to shore. He left his wire cutters on the bank of the aqueduct; he could pick them up later. As for now he wanted both his hands free for the rifle. The ads said it could even shoot underwater, although it was not advised. Visions of his anniversary present rusting away temporarily filled Gus's mind. Well, after the election he would have all the time in the world to clean it.

He moved slowly through the tall marijuana plants toward Trash's main compound. He moved in the direction of the gun barn. The barn was not-so-secretly filled with weapons Trash sold south. Gus stopped short of the barn while still in good cover of the plants in the field. He lay down on the soil and gave the barn a solid examination. He kept hoping the moon would rise and allow him to see well.

Gus could make out a figure slumped in front of the door of the barn. Gus used his rifle site to try to examine the figure. The night was too dark to make out exactly who it was in front of the barn door, but it was clearly a person. Gus stood on the edge of the marijuana field and tossed a few rocks toward the figure. The figure remained slumped in front of the barn. Gus picked up a bigger stone and tossed it in an attempt to hit the figure. It took four tries, but finally a rock plunked off the head of the figure and the figure slid further down the door.

The barn obscured Gus's sight of much of the main house, but it was ideal for sneaking in closer to examine the main goal of the visit: the ranch house. Gus crawled on his belly over to the barn door. The soil was clinging to his wet body. Up close he saw that the crouched figure was poor Johnny Owens. He had a nice bullet hole clean through his heart. The body wasn't too cold to the touch. It was too bad; he at one time had been a nice kid. Gus slowly stood up and decided to try the lock on the barn door. It was still locked. Whoever shot up poor Johnny wasn't interested in Trash's weapon cache. If it was a gang hit, then it was a funny one, leaving all these expensive guns behind. Gus figured that something actually making sense in this case would be unheard of, so the weapons being of no interest must make sense, if only the whole thing made sense. At the moment it didn't.

Gus moved to the edge of the barn and got back down on the ground. He now slid himself down the side of the barn until he got to the corner where he could obtain a good look at the entire main house. He used his rifle scope again to see if there was anything he could make out. The house lights were all off. The driveway was a dark void from this distance. There was no one moving about the compound, but this didn't mean no one was around. They might be waiting for the shooters that hit poor Johnny to make another move. Gus couldn't be sure if the event was over or in the middle of happening. After waiting a few minutes with nothing eventful happening, Gus started to crawl over to the main house.

After about ten feet Gus stopped. Seriously, he thought, what's with all the sneaking? It was time to find out if someone was really around, so Gus stood up. Nothing happened. He walked over to the front porch of the ranch house. There was a figure on the porch in an awkward position that a living person wasn't likely to be in for long. The figure didn't move and Gus ignored it.

Gus went to the front door. It was full of holes but still locked. Gus looked up and saw the porch lights weren't just off. All the outside lights were broken. Probably someone shot them out. Two dead boys and some dead lights; Gus's late night trip to do a little questioning wasn't going very well. No one seemed to be in a talking kind of mood.

Gus went down from the porch and moved around the house until he found he was behind it. He spied a nice low-lying window at the back of the house that made an attractive place to break and enter. It had an old-fashioned lock on it. Gus took the rifle butt and hit the window between the two panes, and the old-style mechanical lock popped open. Getting into an old place like this was stupid easy if you were old enough like Gus to remember how to do it.

Gus slid the window open. He leaned his rifle against the side of the house. No sense having a pointless accident while climbing inside. He then inelegantly hoisted himself through the window.

Gus landed in the Tannehill house with a thud. The loud noise didn't matter, as there apparently was no one left to be alerted. The hard landing left Gus with a pain in his elbow to go with his sore back and cut head. Gus wobbled to his feet and tried to dust the mud off his wet clothes.

Now that he was inside the house, his first task was to locate the front door. Gus had a decent mental picture of the house from the outside and swiftly found the entrance room. Two more figures lay on the ground next to the front door. They looked like they were hit by a weapon that put out a serious amount of rapid fire. The walls around them were well ventilated as well. They had AK-47s lying next to their bodies. It was a nice gun in the hands of a trained expert; unfortunately the trained experts appeared to have been on the other team.

Gus stepped over the bodies and unlocked the front door. He opened it to make sure it was the front entrance to the house. He wasn't taking anything for granted anymore. He closed the bullet-riddled door and left it unlocked. All that was left was to find out if Trash Tannehill was still home.

Gus found Trash in the kitchen. He was bound to a kitchen chair with razor wire. It was a rather cruel thing to do to a man. It was the sort of thing drug gangs did to each other. The razor wire had cut him up good, but that wasn't the cause of death. Trash had seven syringes sticking out of his arm. The plungers were all down. Trash's head was left tilted up with his mouth gaping. His eyes were wide open and dilated. It had probably been a rather thrilling—although short-lived—high. Trash wouldn't be doing any more talking with Gus, that was for certain. Had he known something important or not was now totally irrelevant. Whoever they were, they were ahead of Gus again. Gus felt far behind and out of clues to find his remaining killers. Gus searched Trash's pockets, but they were empty. No more little notes with clues on them.

Gus moved toward the front door to leave his useless dead witnesses when a sound came from outside. A car engine. An automobile was driving up the driveway toward the front of the house. Gus backed away from the front door. It would be better to exit back out his window where his rifle was. Suddenly he was worried he might need it.

As Gus arrived at the window, it exploded from a gunshot. The blast scared Gus and his gut instinct took over. Back down to the floor he dove. He looked up to see his good old friend Trash had purchased expensive bulletproof glass for his crumby old-style windows. The local drug dealers were their own brand of brilliant idiots, which fortunately had just saved Gus's life. Another shot hit the window, and it spider webbed more from cracks. Someone was pissed off they just missed their chance to get rid of Gus. Not a terrible idea: make some noise out front to make Gus moved to the back window, where he'd be a sitting duck. It meant they've been around awhile, watching Gus move about the complex.

Gus moved with all the speed he had in his old body. He figured the shooter couldn't be in two places at once, and if the expert with the gun was in the back waiting for him, he'd move out the front door fast before they could circle around the house. Gus didn't wait to open the door. He lowered his shoulder and hit the unlocked door with a full charge. The door, already weary from the pounding it took from the automatic gunfire earlier in the day, easily broke off its hinges and crashed down, with Gus in tow.

It was a valiant dramatic charge, but for naught, as there was no one on the other side waiting for Gus. There was a car sitting in front of the house with both its front seats empty. The car was probably black or at least dark in color; Gus couldn't be sure with its headlights blaring at him through the dark night, and he wasn't about to double check to make 100 percent sure. Gus popped up surprisingly quick and ran by the automobile and into the marijuana field. He could hear at least one person coming up fast behind him from a distance off. The killer had a good plan, but like Gus they hadn't counted on Trash being an idiot and buying bulletproof glass for a 1920s-style window. Now Gus and the shooter were scrambling in a mad dash, both their carefully made plans for the night completely ruined.

Gus was making for the aqueduct and, hopefully, safety on the neighboring emu farm. The dash was starting to turn into a jog as Gus's body asked him questions, like who did he think he was fooling trying to run a continuous full sprint at his age. His heart was pounding so hard he felt for sure the attack was only a matter of time.

About halfway to the aqueduct, the younger pursuer came close enough to get a shot off and a bullet hit Gus's left leg. Down he went into the field.

A red laser light now cut through the marijuana forest, passing briefly over Gus's head. For a second Gus thought that maybe that truck driver was right and the aliens were actually here. Unfortunately as blood flow returned to his head and Gus reasoned correctly that this wasn't the act of aliens it was a laser targeting system on a killer's rifle. Despite the obscuring forest of plants all around Gus, this killer was doing a decent job of homing in on Gus's location. He probably had infrared goggles on as well. Who were these people that they could wipe out a drug cartel and move on to a local sheriff without batting an eye?

Gus wanted badly to find out, but not exactly at this second. He now moved quickly and very low to the ground. He could hear someone moving through the field, looking for him. Another shot came in Gus's direction, but it hit the plants five feet in front of him. Gus didn't waste time thinking about the close miss. He slid quickly down the bank of the aqueduct and slipped down into the water, making a splash. Gus decided to try to swim underwater and hope the bullets wouldn't penetrate all the way to him. It was a really good plan, but Gus was so out of breath he could barely swim at all, let alone underwater to the other side of the property line.

He made it nonetheless and crawled up the bank of the aqueduct. His face ran into that of a curious emu. Up close the emu was an impressively large bird, and it was now towering over Gus's half-submerged head. This condition was very temporary, as another shot rang out and bird feathers erupted all around Gus. As the bird fell dead next to him, Gus moved away from its body and into the emu-filled field around him.

Infrared goggles were good at spotting Gus in a forest of pot, but let's see how they'd do in a forest of warm-blooded birds, thought Gus. He found a grouping of more or less motionless emus and slid in next to them. He could hear someone moving in the aqueduct water where he came from. The birds ignored Gus, and all their heads seemed to twist in the direction of the person moving in the water. He took out his sidearm. It was wet but it should still be functional. He watch in the direction of the aqueduct and waited.

A few emus were wandering about, probably due to all the noise and commotion. Eventually his friend with the gun would guess at which hot spot in this field was actually him. He waited, hoping they'd guess wrong and he would get a chance to shoot back. Finally he saw the red targeting laser light pointing out from the bank at the direction of an emu. Mist in the air made the laser path clearly visible in the darkness of the moonless night. Gus had a split second to shoot his suspect, but should he shoot to the left of the light or right? Most people were right handed, thought Gus. He should shoot to the right of the laser light. The weapon down by the aqueduct discharged, and Gus, snuggled in nicely by his warm emu friends, fired once in the direction of the light. An emu shrieked somewhere out in the field. Down by the aqueduct Gus heard a splash. The emu farm was a mess of moving and running panicked emus. Gus ducked his head and hoped he didn't get trampled in the commotion erupting around him.

The Dresden house came alive with more lights. There was at least one person on the porch shouting into the field, "Identify yourselves or we'll shoot!"

Gus looked over at the main house. There were about four silhouettes of men on the porch, carrying flashlights and, probably, guns. Gus yelled in as booming voice as he could muster, "Don't worry, it's only your good buddy and local sheriff, Sheriff Gus!"

"What in all hell is going on in my field?" boomed back a voice that Gus knew as Frank Dresden's.

Gus yelled back as honest a lie as he could think of quickly. "I spied some lights in your field when I was doing my ranch-land inspections. I was pretty sure it was that emu rustler I'd been tracking. Looks like I guessed right, because they took a shot at me. If you'd be so kind, could you get your asses over here and help me out?"

Frank and three other young men came down through the field with flashlights to find the bleeding Gus trapped in their angry emu-filled field. They were carrying long poles.

"What are the poles for?" asked Gus.

"You have to be the craziest son of a bitch alive. The poles are for herding the emus. They got big claws on the ends of their toes. They can hurt a man pretty fierce if you're not careful. I can't imagine an idiot running into my emu pen in the middle of the night scaring my birds by shooting off weapons. A man like that has got to have a death wish!"

Gus looked over at his new emu friends. Some of them took a bullet for old Gus. Maybe it was the other company that made them mad, because they had been friendlier to Gus than most people had been all night.

"Well, one of you help me up. I think the snip-...I mean rustler is down by the water."

Frank sent a young hand down with Gus to the aqueduct while he herded the emus away from the area and into their closure pens in the pasture. The young hand was pretty good with a flashlight and soon spotted the body of a black woman slumped backward on the bank of the aqueduct.

"Wow, Sheriff, look at the neat stuff that woman has on. Those night-vision goggles alone run you a pretty penny. Military issue those are. They got better resolution than the crap they sell you in the hunting magazines."

The young lad went over and found her rifle sunk into the black of the aqueduct water. "Wow, I wish I could afford one of these. I'm a collector, and this one is a super nice model. Military issue like this costs way too much for me to afford. I guess rustling emus pays mighty well."

The young man kept talking about guns. Gus sat down on the bank of the aqueduct and cautiously sorted through the body. She had two Glocks tucked into holders around her waist. She had a black outfit with ammo holders sewed in. Despite moving through the water, the fabric had picked up very little water on its surface. Strapped to her back was a fully automatic weapon. There was nothing useful, however, on the body—no ID, no car keys. She was African-American, but Gus couldn't be sure about the American part. She looked fit to say the least. Gus did and didn't know who she was. She was someone's really skilled hired goon. Somewhere else there was a body she was supposed to be guarding.

Gus looked now at the wound in his leg. Not too bad, but it would leave a nasty scar and, worse, would probably turn septic after he swam through the emu waterway. He needed to see a doctor.

"Kid, I think I need a little help limping up to the main house."

The young man seemed reluctant to leave the body and its treasure trove of guns and killing devices. Gus tried to break the spell. "So you collect guns, do you, kid?"

The kid looked brighter upon hearing the question. "You know I do! This here is about the best collection I've ever seen one person carry at one time! It would cost you a pretty penny, that's for sure. But walking around armed like that, not a soul in the world would mess with you. Ain't that right, Sheriff?"

"Well, think of it this way: she collected guns, and right now they're not doing her a lot of good. If I were you, I'd think about starting a stamp collection instead."

CHAPTER 7

Gus was beat. Physically he was clearly beaten. He had been stuck in a hospital bed for a few days, receiving rounds of intravenous antibiotics to his infected leg wound. Mentally he felt he was not actually beaten at all. His mind was as sharp as ever. But, trapped in the little hospital bed, he had little to expend his mind on.

Despite his mental sharpness, the murder case appeared to be headed for a clear loss. Somewhere there was a man that killed or was involved in the killing of a young girl, left two women in the hands of two other thugs, and as an extra bonus had an entire drug compound murdered. Meanwhile Gus was stuck in a bed looking over the latest editions of the county paper. He knew everything in them already, but rereading them helped pass the time.

Gus had been interviewed by the state police twice and wrote out a version of what happened at the ranch. The first official word was probably a drug hit, because no one could think of any other reason why someone would lay waste to a whole drug compound except because it was a drug compound. The black automobile was never recovered, and it was assumed to have departed with the remaining rival drug hitmen. As for the dead hitwoman...well, the federal agencies weren't very forthcoming with much useful information. They said that her fingerprints could be identified, and her real name was Sophia Disraeli, a dentist from Cincinnati.

While Gus didn't like dentists no matter where they came from, he sort of doubted the official version of the identification.

A knock on the room door took Gus away from his paper. Brian Hartline, the commissioner of the state police was standing by the door. He was the man Gus was helping solve the case. Although they had shared this murder case for a while, it was only now did he bother to talk to Gus again. He didn't look happy to be there. Gus couldn't remember ever seeing him happy.

Commissioner Hartline walked up to Gus's bed and gave him a quick look over. "Stupid fucking thing you did up there at the ranch. Too bad you didn't get killed. It is bad luck to die in the line of duty, but it is better than getting killed at the election booth."

"Nice to see you too, Brian. Aren't you going to compliment me for beating your boys to the murderers? If I run across any more lethal dentists in my county, feel free to lend a hand. I am after all only helping you on this case."

"Dentists, right. That's a bunch of horseshit, and we both know it. Fucking federal people playing us for sucks," said Hartline bitterly.

"Do you know which agency it is that's playing games?"

"Who the fuck knows? There are sixty-five different talking-head federal agencies to choose from, so feel free to take your pick. First they covered up the identity of those two thugs you killed, and now they're screwing us on this Tannehill shooting. I wouldn't really care at all if the sucks hadn't called me up and told me to come over here."

"So it's the federal people coming up with those cock-and-bull cover stories. Who called you?"

"I called him," said a new man that appeared at the hospital room door. He was a rather short, ratty-looking man in a suit too tight for his body. He wore a pair of black-rimmed glasses and had a briefcase needlessly handcuffed to his arm. He grabbed a steel-framed chair and dragged it across the floor up to the hospital bed. He then sat down, placing the briefcase on his lap, and unlocked it. He pulled two pieces of paper from the briefcase.

Gus and Brian both remained silent, watching the ratty little man's street theater until the briefcase opened. Then it was a race to see who could complain first.

Commissioner Hartline beat Gus to the punch. "Who the fuck are you and why am I here? I got three dead bodies and a batch of silly stories to tell the public because you people won't tell me anything. So either tell me something useful or fuck off!" The commissioner clearly got to where he was because of his gentle manner and choice words.

The ratty little federal man was composed and didn't appear intimidated. Gus knew who was in charge of the room. The little man handed one piece of paper to Gus and another to the commissioner.

"Are you going to tell me what this piece of paper says, or should I pretend to read it?" asked Gus.

In a rather nice and friendly manner, the federal man explained, "Off the record I can't tell you anything. The three people killed by the sheriff were agents—"

"Ours or theirs?" barked out the commissioner. Gus had no idea who "theirs" referred to, but then he figured neither did the commissioner.

It didn't matter, because the outburst did nothing to slow the federal man's momentum. "And this has caused certain problems in terms of national security. We are sorry for the stonewalling from the government, but that sheet of paper I just handed you contains our official cover story. It is needed, you understand, to protect our agents from harm's way and to protect national security. On the record we are willing to say these suspects were part of a notorious emu-rustling ring well known to the department for years. They were foreign emu agents sent to attack the American emu supply chain. I would like to add one more thing: if the state police and county sheriff won't accept this story, then there will be certain federal troubles."

The little man closed his briefcase and dragged the chair back to where he found it. He then walked out of the room without further acknowledgment of the other two men.

Commissioner Hartline made eye contact with Gus. "Bunch of bullshit crap." He then proceeded to crumble his piece of paper into a ball and bounced it off the wall onto the floor. He frowned at Gus and walked out of the hospital room. Gus was mad that the case remained unofficially satisfactory and officially absolutely silly, but, trapped in a hospital bed, it was the best Gus could do.

Emu rustlers killed attempting to foil a drug hit was the official story on the hospital TV that Gus had to pay an extra two hundred dollars a day to have turned on. It was a surprisingly easy story to tell the public. Gus received flowers, balloons, greeting cards, and even a marriage proposal in congratulations for "solving" the case and freeing the county from fantasy rustlers and drug dealers. Half the well-wishers still thought the two hit-men were sex maniacs, even with the new cover story all over the news.

It showed not everyone was unhappy with the case results. Terrance was happy as could be at Gus's election standing. The polls showed Gus was nearly even with Lance, and Lance's billboards were all coming down with still two weeks before the official voting. His money stream appeared to have suddenly and unexpectedly dried up.

The mayor was less happy with Gus, because now the county's chief buffer to the Mexican drug horde was dead. This didn't last long, though, as Gus told him an unofficial story about how bravely the county boys fought to the bitter end to protect the city from foreign emu agents. The mayor was planning to make the emu the official county bird as a symbol-ism of patriotism.

None of that really mattered to Gus. What did matter to him was, finally he was able to return home. He was walking with a walking stick to compensate for the leg wound, but beside that he was generally all right.

Not that you could just walk out of a hospital. A large woman with a wheelchair had to come to the room and wheel him out. Although they'd just spent two days getting Gus better, he still wasn't good enough to walk out on his own. He never would be well enough for that. Hospitals have got liability that they need to keep in check. He also wasn't allowed to drive home. To Gus's surprise Dr. Armstrong had kindly called him to tell him she was willing to take him home. Gus figured it wasn't in fact to congratu-late him for solving the case or because she was concerned for his health. She just wanted, like everyone else involved in the case, to blow off steam.

Gus sat in a wheelchair outside the lobby, waiting for Dr. Armstrong to pick him up. She drove a little subcompact that ran on natural gas. (Gus had no idea what the difference between natural and unnatural gas was. He would leave that subject a mystery.) He hobbled over to the car and opened the door. Then they were off toward Gus's home. They were silent for a block or two. Gus was just waiting for the volcano to erupt.

Dr. Armstrong finally spoke. "What is really going on? I can't believe anything I read in the papers or see on television. The official storyline is complete fantasy. You got to know that too. So are you going to let me in on it?"

Gus told her what he was supposed to tell her. "There are some things in law enforcement you just have to accept. The bad guys are dead, so what does it matter how and why they died?"

"But are they all dead?" asked Dr. Armstrong, watching too much of Gus and not enough of the road for Gus's liking.

She wasn't happy; perhaps they were the only two in the county not truly happy with the outcome. Part of the public had two dead sex maniacs, part of them had dead rustlers, part of them had dead drug dealers, and some of them had a dead dentist. All together they were happy at the idea of any of those four being dead.

Gus thought all in all Chloe was an improvement to the coroner's office. He liked her. He liked that she wasn't happy, but he couldn't tell her that.

"Can't kill all the bad people, or there'd be no one left. I think we got rid of the principle agents involved, and beyond that for the time being there isn't anything else to do. Eventually the really bad people will commit some other stupid crime and get caught. They can't help themselves. People don't always go to jail for the worst thing they've ever done. You'll just have to be dissatisfied with that idea," said Gus, not really convinced.

"I don't believe that," said Dr. Armstrong.

Gus looked over to her. What more needed to be said? They drove the rest of the way in silence. She left him off in the driveway. She was nice enough to offer assistance inside, knowing he wouldn't accept it. Gus didn't and that was the end of it.

There were newspapers lying on Gus's doormat when he got to the front door. He painfully bent over to pick them up. He threw them in the garbage, as he didn't need to read them.

Gus was still weak from the blood loss and the infection that had followed. After a quick dinner, he decided it was best to catch an early bedtime. He barely had the energy to take off his clothes and crawl into bed. Tomorrow was a new day, and he still had two solid weeks on an even playing field to win his job back. He shut off the lights and went to sleep.

Gus's bedroom was dark. It was late in the evening and yet there was a shadow moving through the bedroom. The figure moved about effortlessly even without the lights on. The figure stood at the foot of the bed. He touched a screen on the flat panel he was holding in his hand and the lights in the room turned on. Gus grumbled in his bed and reluctantly rose slightly on his pillow, still not fully aware of the unwelcome visitor's presence nor of why his room lights were suddenly on.

The mysterious figure was wearing a Guy Fawkes mask. The masked man slid off the infrared glasses he was wearing. He spoke to Gus loudly but calmly so that Gus would realize he was not alone. "Rise up, my good friend. I have come because I want to have a final word with you before we must, sadly, depart."

Gus glanced at the analog alarm clock by his bedside. It was confirming the time as the middle of the night. Some idiot was shining the room lights in his face when all he wanted to do was sleep. Gus's tired eyes had trouble putting anything into focus. He was pretty sure at the foot of his bed stood a well-built man wearing a goofy mask. The man was holding a digital device in one hand and a revolver in the other.

"I'm too drowsy to have a little chat with anyone. Now do me a favor and turn off my lights or shoot me. I don't care which you choose, but I just am not in the mood tonight for late-night talking with a lunatic."

The man spoke in a pseudo-dramatic voice. "Lunatic? Don't you recognize the face of Guy Fawkes when you see it? Your lights; aren't they great? I rigged up your lights to the Internet. Now with just a simple touch of my pad I can turn them on and off. It's the future, Sheriff." The masked man proceeded to turn the lights on and off in rapid fashion by touching the pad with the thumb of his gun-holding hand.

Gus didn't care and was too tired to fake it. "Wow, that's really great. I was worried mister Gay Fox had woken me up in the middle of the night for no good reason other than to kill me face to face, and here it was all the time you just wanted me to see that electrician's spectacle."

The man removed his mask to reveal the face of a blond man in his late thirties or possibly forties. He was a pretty good-looking guy. "Oh please, my good friend, let's not joke about revolutionaries. I'm not here to take a shot at you. I might give you a shot, but I'd never take one. I'm neither a thief nor a shooter by trade, despite what they might say about me. I'm a hacker by trade, as you know or don't you know. I've seen on the nightly news that you do not have it all figured out yet. I'm sorry about that, but important people are helping me as best they can to remain mysteriously unknown. It is too bad this place is no longer safe for me, as I was enjoying myself immensely here. But, alas, try as we might to hush up this affair with the young woman, too many people have now talked; that drug man talked, that little girl talked, and our shell company somehow talked. We tried to close as many loopholes as we could for the sake of my secrecy, but it didn't work. My keepers are, I think, on the whole very ungrateful people on this subject. They have complained bitterly that I lived a reckless life when I was supposed to remain incognito. As if they didn't know what kind of life I led when they hired me. I have left too long a trail, so away I must go. They try so hard to make me feel kind of guilty about this whole affair. It's silly, isn't it?"

"Well, congratulations on not giving into their guilt trip. Since you want to chat, could I clarify who exactly killed who? I got the two professional killers in the silver car as almost certainly the killers of Pam, from whom they were forcing information about where you were. Not that she knew. Now Trash, I imagine, was killed by the people trying to protect you. Everyone thought he knew something, but what it was he knew I imagine only you now know. Your highly trained dentist from Cincinnati or government-owned bodyguard spent that night trying to eliminate me as well. Waste of time, because I don't know who the fuck you are. I still don't!"

The figure put a forefinger to his lips. "Shhh. Good, because no one is supposed to know. That is the whole part of anonymity. The life of being a faceless unknown is a boring one. I loved the old life I had as an underground hacker, with its drugs, women, fame, and the challenge. I must admit from time to time I put on disguises and have my fun outside of my hiding spot. My handlers didn't like it, but I am highly valuable to them, so I get to do as I please so long as I do my work well. In a way it is all fun and games.

"Too bad I met a series of people that are not so easily fooled. They saw through my little disguises. This girl told me that she knew I was not Captain Jacob Hancock, international monetary trader—but she didn't tell me this then when we first met. If she had, I would have walked away into the crowd and remained unknown. That's how this should have ended, had she been honest with me at our first meeting. But people in this world are so dishonest. She waited to tell me she knew I was lying about my identity until we were all alone in my place. My place, which is supposed to be a secret!"

Gus remained sitting up in the bed, trying to use his pillow to prop his body up. "Did Trash see through it too?"

"I don't know. We killed him because too many people were talking. He wrote things down about us and looked into our money fronts, my little operational company to help me live better. I am a very good hacker and I covered my tracks very well, but I do not like people snooping into my private business. Those stalkers got information from him, and my life was in real danger from those two. So we killed Trash, but, I fear, too late, and now my poor company shall have to go bankrupt. It doesn't really matter. As one institution goes down, another one can quickly be put up again."

Gus rubbed his temples and asked. "So you killed everyone in attempt to keep them quiet?"

"You really aren't very good at your job, are you? I've read the official story from the police. A greater piece of fiction I have never read, and I've read a lot of bullshit in my time. The Internet is filled with stories of people claiming to have seen me. Some of them are true, some are not.

Many of them, I must admit, I wrote myself just to have a little fun. I do deserve a little fun."

"Do you really think I'd kill a beautiful girl because she knew who I was? We were doing heroin and she started to convulse. She fell off the bed and broke her neck. A dead body is not an easy story to cover up. But we tried! We drugged the two others, and my professional help cleaned the place and stashed the body."

Gus was getting a good story, but was it just another story? Gus wanted to keep him talking and not shooting, so he asked him another question. "So why Lance Daniels?"

The man laughed. "That bastard was bought good and cheap, wasn't he? He was supposed to be insurance to keep me safe and warm in your county. Do you think I want to keep moving from town to town? It's helpful to own the local sheriff, as you know already. But then that bitch dies, a few hitmen showed up, and that bastard drug dealer tries to sell my story to whomever he can sell it to. They ruined everything. Those hitmen kill another girl, for which I am sorry, but what could I do? I need to stay quiet and safe. I can't stick around here anymore. I don't need to control the local sheriff's office now, because we're moving on."

"That all sounds fine to me. Who were the two hitmen working for?" asked Gus. He figured as long as he kept the man talking in circles, he might reveal something truthful and stop making excuses.

"We don't know. Russian mafia, hired by European bankers or possibly hired by some Middle East oil baron. I've hacked and attacked them all. The establishment does not go down easy. Their arrival here was just an unfortunate coincidence. Maybe they were drawn by the mysterious death, or perhaps my fun left too many trails for them to follow. It doesn't matter; you cleaned them up nicely for me." The figure bowed a thank you to Gus.

Gus was put off. "I'm not sure you owe me a thank you."

The figure waved him off. "But I do, I do thank you from the bottom of my heart. You've cleaned up everything, even the problem of what to do with my little helper. She knew too much, don't you think? She knew where all the bodies were, so to speak. It's better to start with fresh handlers in a new place."

Gus held up his hand to persuade him to wait. "Are you going to tell me who you are before you leave me?"

The figure shook his head in dissatisfaction. "You think you're clever. You think that here in your county was some grand mystery to solve. You tried to solve it, but for *your* benefit, not for your citizens. You want me to give you the ultimate ending, but I don't give information out for free, you know. I hack for my information. Other hackers and whistleblowers give it to me, information that has a lot of value to certain people. They, as you know, will kill to keep it a secret. The control of information has a very high price. The lack of information can help control people. The freeing of it can free people. They hide this information because they know free information will shatter the earth as we know it! I'm the guy that runs the sites that allows the freed information to shatter the earth. What they call my enterprise depends on the nature of the information. Every freedom fighter is another man's terrorist. Espionage and treason, certain people with power call it. *Total information awareness*, the professors in colleges call it. I like to think of myself as an information libertarian."

"Aw crap," rolled off Gus's lips. Gus's mind trained back to his disjointed conversation with Nigel Laurence. He waved that stupid flat screen at him. There was a website on the screen, the most popular website on campus, he had said. Everyone his age knew who Josh Hansen was. Apparently even Cherry Colston. He was a mysterious Internet figure that fought a fight only people of that age seem to understand. He was loved and hated. The Internet allowed him to be anywhere. And that apparently included at the foot of Gus's bed.

"Are you really so important that people are paid to handle you? Please tell me why a person so interested in freedom has allowed himself to be bound down. It would appear every piece of information in your world is fair game but that which is about you. Doesn't seem fair, does it?"

The man frowned in disapproval. As he spoke his voice got louder and angrier. "I am not handled! I handle them. Do you understand? Yes, people come to me and give me information. I free the information so the masses can know the truth. Only a mushroom grows in the dark, my friend. Society can't grow so long as these governments exist and these authoritarian men can hide behind the veil of secrecy. The leakers used to go to the press with their information, but far too often these days the press is already bought and sold. So now they come to me, because they know I will release any and all the mushrooms to the light. I believe in this world and its beautiful people. I believe they are allowed to know the truth no matter what it is. When we have all been made equal because we know everyone's secrets, we will no longer need these puppet governments."

It occurred to Gus that he didn't care. One excuse for murdering a bunch of people didn't seem better than any other. His goal was to keep him talking and not shooting, so he asked another question. "Until this time comes, you are allowing yourself to play the puppet?"

The man held his hands out wide in another melodramatic gesture. "What can I say? I pulled the wrong strings too many times. The people with money do not like me. They want my site destroyed. They can't out-hack me, so they try to destroy my life. For every winner there has to be an information loser. So I play games and get a puppet government to protect me. They do not understand the world like I understand it."

Gus yawned. He was tired and he just couldn't help it. The fake figure in his bedroom was boring him. "There is nothing I like more after being shot at than a night of someone telling me how much more important they are than me. Can we skip to the end?"

Josh pointed the gun at Gus with both hands. "I came here to accuse you, Sheriff. I show that the system that they claim is flawless and fair is nothing but a flimsy house of cards. You are a pawn in that house. And I subtract cards one by one. My handlers think they control me. They don't understand that when I have removed enough cards, the whole house will fall down. It will not be just their enemies' houses, but the whole house that comes down. Then people like you, Sheriff, that have enabled them so long, shall be crushed in the collapse. The people that served and protected the system will be burned at the stake by the angry citizens you fooled."

"I'm just a county sheriff. No one sends me the memos saying which girls' lives are important and which ones aren't. But let's just pretend I understand and have bought into your total information awareness thing. Would you be so kind and tell me: did you intend to kill Cherry Colston or not? It is the only information I really care about tonight. It's late, I'm tired, and frankly you aren't as interesting a person as you think you are."

The man smirked a little. "Now you are having me on, Sheriff. I have given all the information I want to give. If I did kill her, so what? You killed three people and no one is putting you in jail. If you still need more, what can I tell you? I've been busy these past few days. I am a great hacker, and now I have all your cases of racial profiling, I have all the times you harassed and bullied the young, I've got all the out-of-state drivers you needlessly pulled over because you needed to write some tickets to pay your salary. I have the deeper corruption too: the ties to drug dealers, kick-backs from contractors, and all the crimes and misdemeanors you ignored because the person was considered important. Of the two of us, you're the much more corrupt man, Sheriff. You tell me you never got the memo on who is worth it in society and who isn't? Lies. I've hacked your system, I've got it all, and it says to me you've been looking the other way and pre-judging criminals for your whole career. You're as big a hypocrite as you claim that I am, and a very dumb hypocrite at that. I got everything. The whole you, so I don't need to shoot you. I shall destroy you by freeing your information to the public."

"You mean everything? All my emails, all my cases, and all my private communications?"

"Everything," stressed Hansen in a melodramatic voice.

Gus slid his head back on his pillow. "Well, then I guess you win. Can you turn the lights out so I can go back to sleep?"

"Sure. But don't get all brave and try to take the information back. Rest assured, I have plenty of backups." He threw an information storage device at Gus just to stress the point it would do no good for Gus to try anything.

"Now don't get all sore and mean at me. Really just go away, please. I ain't brave and I know when I'm beat. So you go total information me out of business. Just don't bore me any more tonight. The only thing I want to know in the world tonight you're too chicken to tell me. We both know the answer anyways. The whole world is full of hypocrites, so I don't see who is going to be left when the house of cards actually collapses. We're both hypocrites fighting to keep our jobs. The only difference is, I've always known it."

Hansen was angry again. "You understand nothing, my friend, and by the end of tomorrow the citizens of this county will be demanding you go to jail. Whereas tomorrow I will be somewhere beautiful with the freedom to enjoy myself as I please. Think of what I am going to do to you as a small lesson as to what I am doing to the world. The same lesson dictators, lying scientists, generals, torturers, and corrupt bankers have already learned. You are nothing compared to them, just a cog in their machine. But every cog removed helps topple the machine, my sheriff friend. I will enjoy watching from afar as you get your lesson."

Gus slid back up on his pillow. "Since we're doing lessons, I'll give you one right back. You just remember some words of advice that my daddy always told me: Don't ever think it is enough to be the goose that lays the golden egg. Eventually the goose gets good and fat from living too easy a comfortable life. A golden-egg-laying goose is expensive to keep up, and above all else a farmer still needs to eat. One day the fat old gold-laying goose starts to make too much of a nuisance of itself, and the farmer says, 'Fuck it. People may love gold with all their heart, but when push comes to shove, you can't eat it.' Every goose, even the gold-laying one, eventually gets cooked."

Hansen laughed and then touched his screen with his thumb. The room plunged into darkness. He could hear a man running away. Gus stayed in bed. The idiot thought he was going to go after him. Every self-important moron is the same. How many shots does the man think Gus wants taken at him during one investigation? Gus learned all he was going to learn already. Getting out of bed wasn't going to tell him anything more.

Hansen wasn't going to jail. Not tonight and probably not ever. But eventually his goose was going to be cooked.

The papers already thought the case was solved. Now it was as solved as it ever was going to be. It was over. Corrupt stories about sheriffs are a dime a dozen, and there was too much information on those files. What story would Marty and his like find among all that information? Corruption, like Hanson hoped? Possibly.

Or maybe they would carve out the story of a hard-working small-county sheriff. They'd find an old man worried about living alone after his wife's death. A man fighting for a county that was falling by the wayside in the new postindustrial era. Hansen would release everything, but someone else would tell the readers what it all meant. A lot of those someones shared Gus's experience in this county and didn't give a crap for the opinions of outsiders like Hansen.

Gus had learned one thing from this case: information, even the free kind, was impossible to control. The story would flow the way it would flow, and Hansen couldn't guarantee it flowed against Gus. Indeed, sometimes even the most negative stories found public support. It was only a few weeks until the election, and who was the public going to prefer: the sheriff who foiled the emu-rustling dentist ring, who was onsite to see the local drug gang's demise, and who killed the two sex maniac kidnappers? Or Lance Daniels, the penniless monkey to a machine that had just skipped town?

Gus effortlessly fell back to sleep.